Remembering last night,
Laini managed not to sigh aloud.

She'd been swept up, like Dorothy and Toto in a
Kansas tornado, in a sweet fantasy of how it might
be for D.J. and her—for D.J., young Murphy and
her—if she were to let the emotions that churned
inside her have their way. If she and D.J. were to let
Murphy's yearning to make them a family actually
happen.

It might, if she wasn't careful, Laini thought. She
could fall in love with D.J.; she felt halfway in love
with him already, and she nearly drowned in his eyes
every time their glances met.

But she mustn't let it happen. Falling in love with
D.J. would be a disaster.

Dear Reader:

Happy October! The temperature is crisp, the leaves on the trees are putting on their annual color show and the daylight hours are getting shorter. What better time to cuddle up with a good book? What better time for Silhouette Romance?

And in October, we've got an extraspecial lineup. Continuing our DIAMOND JUBILEE celebration is Stella Bagwell—with *Gentle as a Lamb*. The wolf is at shepherdess Colleen McNair's door until she meets up with Jonas Dobbs—but is he friend or the ultimate foe? Only by trusting her heart can she tell for sure.... Don't miss this wonderful tale of love.

The DIAMOND JUBILEE—Silhouette Romance's tenth anniversary celebration—is our way of saying thanks to you, our readers. To symbolize the timelessness of love, as well as the modern gift of the tenth anniversary, we're presenting readers with a DIAMOND JUBILEE Silhouette Romance each month, penned by one of your favorite Silhouette Romance authors. In the coming months, writers such as Lucy Gordon and Phyllis Halldorson are writing DIAMOND JUBILEE titles especially for you.

And that's not all! There are six books a month from Silhouette Romance—stories by wonderful writers who time and time again bring home the magic of love. During our anniversary year, each book is special and written with romance in mind. October brings you *Joey's Father* by Elizabeth August—a heartwarming story with a few surprises in store for the lovely heroine and rugged hero—as well as *Make-believe Marriage*—Carole Buck's debut story in the Silhouette Romance line. *Cimarron Rebel* by Pepper Adams, the third book in the exciting CIMARRON STORIES trilogy, is also coming your way this month! And in the future, work by such loved writers as Diana Palmer, Annette Broadrick and Brittany Young is sure to put a smile on your lips.

During our tenth anniversary, the spirit of celebration is with us year-round. And that's all due to you, our readers. With the support you've given to us, you can look forward to many more years of heartwarming, poignant love stories.

I hope you'll enjoy this book and all of the stories to come. Come home to romance—Silhouette Romance—for always!

Sincerely,

Tara Hughes Gavin
Senior Editor

ADELINE McELFRESH

Sycamore Point

Silhouette Romance

Published by Silhouette Books New York

America's Publisher of Contemporary Romance

SILHOUETTE BOOKS
300 E. 42nd St., New York, N.Y. 10017

ISBN: 0-373-08750-0

First Silhouette Books printing October 1990

Printed in the U.S.A.

Books by Adeline McElfresh

Silhouette Romance

If Dreams Were Wild Horses #618
Sycamore Point #750

ADELINE McELFRESH

lives in rural southern Indiana, where she pursues her dream: writing, reading, walking, generally enjoying life. She collects old medical books, early American "home cures" and housekeeping hints, colloquialisms. Author of numerous romance and suspense novels published under her own name and pseudonyms, she is a former hospital public relations director, newspaper reporter and editor.

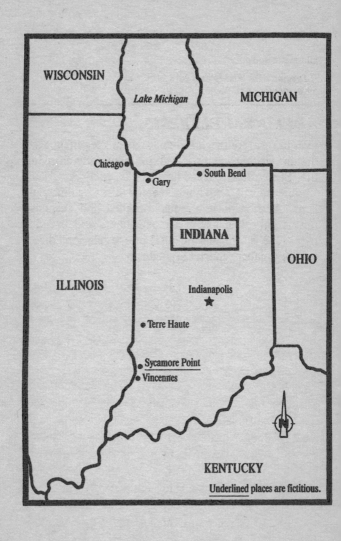

WISCONSIN

Lake Michigan

MICHIGAN

Chicago •

• South Bend
• Gary

INDIANA

ILLINOIS

Indianapolis
★

OHIO

• Terre Haute

• Sycamore Point
• Vincennes

N

KENTUCKY

Underlined places are fictitious.

Chapter One

"Want to see my frog?"

Wearing ragged cut-off jeans and a grungy T-shirt, the skinny, red-haired boy looked as wary of the woman standing in front of him as did the frog he held out to her in both hands.

Laini smiled—valiantly. "Love to," she replied, holding out a hand, palm up, fingers curled. "What's its name?"

"Better use both hands, like I'm doing." Solemn blue eyes met her brown ones. "And it's a he. His name's Frog." An assortment of freckles moved around on his ruddy, thin face as though he were considering a grin. "Caught him in one of them pools down by the river. Glen said I could keep him."

Bracing herself, Laini cupped her hands to form a nest for the frog the way the boy had. She even man-

aged not to flinch when he deposited the frog in it.
"I'm glad you like the river."

He hadn't said he did, but wasn't every child enchanted with a river? She and her brother, Glen, had
loved the Wabash when they were growing up. All
sorts of fantasies had frolicked in her imagination.
Her restlessness had started later, and then she'd
barely been able to wait until she could get away from
the small town.

But she had found herself missing the soft whisper
of the wind in the sycamore trees that grew on the
banks of the Wabash, the smells of the river, the glint
of sunlight on running water. She didn't like to think
how many times she had wakened in the middle of the
night yearning for the sights and sounds of home.

"I had fun on the river when I was your age," she
confided, smiling at the boy again.

"You gonna keep us?"

"Keep you?" Surprised, Laini spoke without
thinking. Hastily she tried to erase the hurt that all of
a sudden was etched across the young face before her.
"Us?"

"Me and Frog. Glen said—" The boy swallowed
what sounded suspiciously like a choked sob, although not a hint of tears shone in his eyes. "Me and
Frog, we ain't got no place nor nobody else."

Oh, my God, Laini thought. Her self-possession
started to crumble. What had Glen promised the child,
anyway?

"Let's not worry about it now," she said gently, lowering her eyes from the boy's penetrating gaze to the frog in her hands. It regarded her unblinkingly.

"Frog likes you," the boy ventured.

"You know," she said, "I think it does."

Curling her fingers a bit more, she touched their tips to the frog's greenish-brown back, half expecting the critter to use its powerful back legs to propel itself out of her hands.

When it didn't, the child's earnest expression blossomed, and Laini saw the first sign of a smile on his face since he'd popped around the corner of the house. "See? He likes you!"

Laini stroked a fingertip over the frog's cool, faintly abrasive skin. She would have loved to ask the boy how long he'd been here and what Glen had told him. But this didn't seem to be the time.

Two days before, a small plane piloted by her brother had crashed into a mountainside in the Smokies while on a flight to Atlanta. She was home to make funeral plans, sell the house where she and Glen had grown up, and find homes for the strays that her brother—with his heart as big as all outdoors—would have taken in in the near year-long time since he'd returned to Sycamore Point.

Remembering how crazy she had thought the move was, Laini sighed. What an incredible waste for a man as gifted as Glen to bury himself in a town like Sycamore Point, Indiana, which wasn't even a wide place in a road going somewhere. Their father had made that mistake, hanging on to a tiny weekly newspaper long after it had become an albatross around his neck.

Glen used to laugh at Laini when she pointed that out, although he had always agreed that their father had possessed the talent and skills to have succeeded anywhere. It had been a long time before Glen had told her he'd always planned to return before he was too old to enjoy Sycamore Point—which was the reason he had insisted they keep the house, the clapboard building that held the decrepit newspaper equipment, and the acres upon acres of woodland along the river. After their father's death, she and Glen had owned it in joint tenancy. It was all hers now, she realized unhappily.

Hers, when she didn't want it.

Poor Glen, she thought, biting her lip. How he had loved every stick and brick in the old house—in the whole town. Unlike her, Glen had found leaving Sycamore Point to be a traumatic experience but, he'd realized, a necessary one if he were to realize his ambition.

And then he had come home. She felt maudlin just thinking about it—and a little puzzled that it had happened so soon.

"I'll live the life of Riley, Sis," he had written her in one of his rare letters, this one shortly before he quit his job. "Regress to my heart's content. Do a little writing and a lot of dreaming. Dad was right. There's something to be said for the slow, easy, more simple life. Sometimes I'm sorry I ever left it."

When she hadn't been able to reach him by phone, Laini had fired off an express-mail letter telling him she thought he was a certifiable lunatic, and to call her before he abandoned a career that hadn't gone, and wouldn't go, anywhere but up.

He hadn't called her, of course.

Next time she heard from him, he was in Sycamore Point and planning to resurrect the small weekly newspaper they'd mothballed when their father died of a massive heart attack. It'd been only a year after their mother's death, and both she and Glen had been in college.

Glen, she remembered, hearing his voice again as he'd told her he was all settled in, had sounded as happy as a June bug.

Now, as then—that November day almost a year earlier—a pang nibbled at Laini. Glen had been the easygoing one of them, she the one with the fire and drive.

And yet, she couldn't help thinking, Glen had been every bit as successful as she . . . and had made it seem so easy. Even his return to Sycamore Point had seemed so natural and right—though, in the back of her mind, premature; but natural and right—for Glen.

She wondered, now, if there'd been something he hadn't told her.

Aware of the boy's scrutiny, she passed the frog back to him, smiling to herself at the care with which he handled it. An instant later his gaze was back on her face. He looked as though he wanted to speak but couldn't find the words, she noticed. She wished he didn't appear so hungry for someone to love him and his frog.

Because she knew her brother's habits, the hound with beseeching eyes and the passel of pups that had greeted her first hadn't been a surprise. All his life Glen had brought home hurt, helpless creatures— many of them injured, others lost or simply unwanted—and had kept them until they could be returned to their natural habitat or he could find a home for them.

But the presence of the boy had surprised her. Probably alerted by the sound of her car, he had dashed around a corner of the rambling old house as she'd stood looking at the familiar scene, feasting her eyes, really; nearly drowning in nostalgia when she had thought she'd put foolish sentimentality behind her, years before.

How wrong she had been.

At her first glimpse of the boy, she had been reminded of the pathetic children in the documentary film she'd just completed—the one that was going to earn her the network job she wanted so badly; and was almost sure of getting, she thought, her self-confidence momentarily sweeping aside the sympathy she felt for the young boy and clouding her feelings of grief and shock at Glen's death. The network brass had liked her tapes....

Remorse darted through her. Glen was her only brother—all the family she had except some distant cousins she had never seen and rarely heard from. How could she think of her career at a time like this?

Fighting the pain, she forced her eyes to meet the child's solemn gaze. She would have to deal with him as she did with Glen's other strays, she told herself firmly: work in a calm, dispassionate manner to find a home for him; not let him find his way into her heart.

It would probably be harder, she mused ruefully as she recalled some of the lessons she had learned while doing her documentary, than finding a home for the dog and the seven appealing puppies that now romped awkwardly around her feet.

D. J. Boone pulled the door shut behind him and stood on the unpaved sidewalk looking at the black-outlined gilt lettering on the plate-glass window, the only new feature of the weathered clapboard building.

N.P.A.S.
(Nostalgia, Pure and Simple)
Glen Moran
Editor, Publisher, Writer,
Typesetter and Printer's Devil

Glen's dream. Back to his roots after ten years of being, in D.J.'s opinion, the best investigative reporter Washington had seen in a long time.

Shoving a rolled copy of the paper into his back pocket, D.J. shook himself mentally. Glen had just begun to get the little publication off the ground. He had mailed out issue 1, volume 1, only hours before taking off for Atlanta, D.J. had learned since his own arrival in Sycamore Point the previous day. Talk about fate taking a hand in a man's life....

Heaving a sigh, D.J. started walking, wondering what business Glen had had in Atlanta. And flying—D.J. scowled at that. Glen had bought the plane a month before at a government auction, according to his housekeeper who'd said, "Glen told my Harley it was a real bargain. Harley said he guessed it had belonged to some drug runner."

"Likely," D.J. had agreed. He knew about those auctions of seized property.

That Glen hadn't mentioned the plane during their phone conversation a couple of weeks before bothered him. Although Glen had been a skilled pilot when they met, seven or eight years before, to D.J.'s knowledge he'd never owned a plane. And Glen had claimed, of late, that he was sick of rushing through life as if he wanted out of it.

"No more running to catch planes or fighting city traffic for me," Glen had declared vehemently on the eve of leaving Washington. "From here on, the sun's going to shine warm in my face and the wind be at my back."

Remembering, D.J. frowned into the late-afternoon sun.

Something wasn't right. Glen had acted as though he thought he had it made here in Sycamore Point. The couple of times D.J. had visited during the past several months, he'd found his friend basking in the glow he'd predicted for himself, apparently as happy as a cow in clover. Buying an airplane—even dirt cheap at a government auction, D.J. reflected now— didn't fit the pattern.

Neither, for that matter, did Glen's idea to adopt an eight-year-old kid.

D.J. shook his head at that. He hadn't even known the boy was in Glen's life, until yesterday. The last time D.J. had visited, in July, Glen had made no mention of the child. Although, knowing Glen, he shouldn't have been surprised, he realized. Glen had a soft spot for the downtrodden; one of his Pulitzers had been for a series of articles on underprivileged children in Marazán, a little country down in Central America. And, from all D.J. gathered, you couldn't get more downtrodden than Murphy Gonzales had been when Glen found him.

Even that, of course, didn't explain why Glen hadn't mentioned the boy the last time they'd talked.

Dragging the copy of *Nostalgia, Pure and Simple* out of his back pocket, he wondered what would happen to Murphy now. And what would happen to the old house? To *Nostalgia, Pure and Simple*?

Glen had only a sister, and she lived on the West Coast. The last time he'd heard Glen speak of her, she'd been working on television documentaries. Laini was an ambitious woman who, Glen had said, speaking fondly, thought he was nuts for harboring his dream of someday going home again.

D.J. doubted she would want to keep the house. For sure, she wouldn't want the dinky little nostalgia sheet;

it was a long way from being anything but a labor of
love.

And he was doubly certain she wouldn't want to
take on a kid of mixed Mexican Irish-American an-
cestry who, according to Glen's housekeeper, didn't
know where either parent was or where he'd been
born. If the boy knew who had brought him to Sycamore Point and abandoned him, Miss Annie had observed wryly, he wasn't telling.

Shaking his head at the puzzle Murphy presented,
D.J. continued toward the Moran place. The silence
was broken by the gleeful barking of Fruitful's pups,
up ahead at the house.

Half smiling at the carefree sound, he tried to sup-
press his own yearning to spend the rest of his days in
a place like this. Despite the still-green trees and grass
as the season pushed toward winter, it reminded him
of the west Texas town he'd grown up in—when he
hadn't been in one of the many boarding schools his
mother had shipped him off to after his father had left
them.

It was like trying to turn off a dripping faucet. The
hunger remained, lurking in the back of his mind and
picking away at his common sense, which advised him
to forget it. He knew he wouldn't forget it.

Glen wasn't the only one who had felt his creative
juices drying up as he raced to stay ahead of the pack
in Washington, D.J. reflected. Glen was simply the
one of them who had taken the bull by the horns and
headed back to what Glen had called ''God's coun-

try'' with such fervor that D.J. had been inclined then—and was inclined now—to agree with him.

Sycamore Point could be good for a man's soul, he decided as he walked on toward the Moran house, its irregular roofline visible now through the trees that surrounded it. He had spent the previous night in the room Glen had told him last Christmas—on his first visit, shortly after Glen's move from D.C.—was his any time and for however long he wanted it. The serenity of the old place, mingled with the sense of Glen's presence, had taken the bitter, angry edge off his grief for a good friend lost too soon.

Yes, he mused, thinking of how Glen had felt about his hometown, a man could make a good life for himself in Sycamore Point—a heck of a lot better than he could sitting behind a video display terminal in a crowded, bustling newsroom editing somebody else's copy, which was what he had been doing when someone yelled out that Glen Moran had been killed in a plane crash.

God, he thought now, he'd never forget the feeling he'd experienced when he'd heard that announcement. It was as if a fist had slammed into his gut. He and Glen Moran had been through a lot together.

"Me and Frog's room's the one right next to Glen's," Murphy volunteered, struggling to carry one of Laini's bags and hold on to Frog at the same time. "Right acrost from D.J.'s." D.J., he had already explained, was Glen's friend; which she knew although she'd never met the man. "Glen brung his old 'quarium down from the attic for Frog."

"I bet Frog feels right at home," Laini said, juggling her other luggage and the portable computer she never went anywhere without.

"Yeah. Glen fixed him a sandbar and everything."

Laini smiled as she pictured her brother making a bullfrog at home in that old fish tank, which was as big as the kitchen table. Her heart constricted. She still had trouble accepting that Glen was gone.

Before she got her emotions under control again, something large and feathered swooshed past her head, clacking its beak. Laini almost dropped everything.

"What," she gasped, "was that?"

"Don't be scared. That's Owl. He wants to eat Frog."

"Frog is in your hand, not in my ear." That snapping beak had been a little too close for comfort.

Warily she watched the large gray bird settle on the back of a chair and regard her with round eyes that gleamed amber in the late-afternoon light that filtered in through a stained-glass window at the end of the hall. She didn't have to ask what an owl was doing in the house; she knew. It was one of Glen's foundlings being nursed back to health.

Breathing more easily, she asked, "What's wrong with it?" The way the bird had zipped past her without making more than a whisper of sound except for that warning click of its beak, seemed to indicate that nothing much was the matter.

"Broken wing," the boy answered.

He'd told her his name was Murphy Gonzales: "Guess my mom named me, 'cause they say her name was Murphy 'fore she met my dad." There was a wistfulness in his tone that touched Laini. "Me and Glen, we was gonna take him down to the river when Glen got back and turn him loose."

"The way it flew past my head, that sounds like a good idea." Why did she feel ashamed of herself for saying that? Laini wondered. She knew how her brother felt about wild creatures.

The look Murphy gave her plainly questioned her sensitivity, although she doubted Murphy had ever heard the word, much less knew its meaning. "Glen said Owl would know when his wing was strong enough to fly away to the woods."

Smiling, Laini agreed, "I'm sure he will." She tightened her grip on her garment bag. "Does Owl have a carrier?"

She wasn't about to carry that wicked-beaked bird under her arm, she thought, casting a glance at the owl as it flexed its huge wings and refolded them against its sides. The round eyes neither blinked nor left her face.

Still cradling the frog to his chest, Murphy narrowly missed banging the bag he carried in his other hand against a claw-footed, marble-topped table on which stood a hand-painted lamp that had belonged to her great-grandmother. Laini cringed.

Peering up at her, Murphy answered, "Yes'm, he's got a cage. But Glen never made him stay in it unless

Miss Annie's here. Glen said Owl needs to fly free, so's his wing'd heal." A grin crept across his freckled face. "Miss Annie said she wasn't having no bird swooping at her when she was cooking and cleaning."

"I can just hear her," Laini said, grateful for a moment's respite. Murphy obviously had adored Glen. Sympathy for the child washed through her, stirring her own grief.

Setting the garment bag down on the floor, she opened the door to the room that had been hers since she could remember.

Instantly nostalgia rushed out, enfolding her in memories she didn't need right now. She'd been happy here, in this room, this house, this town.

Here, she had dreamed the bright and shining dreams that had shaped her life; here, she had shared them with Glen. And she'd listened to his aspirations—as ambitious as her own.

Now she was the only one left.

And she was home in sorrow.

Biting her bottom lip before the tremor she felt building inside her got out of hand, she picked up the garment bag and carried it and her other things into the room. Murphy struggled along at her heels with the bag that was too large for his small stature if not for his determination.

"Maybe," she began, setting her things down and letting her gaze roam the familiar, spacious bedroom, "if we leave the front door open, Owl will fly out."

"We do that," Murphy said matter-of-factly, "and Fruitful and the pups'll be in before you know it."

Laini smiled. He was probably right.

Carefully Murphy placed the bag he had carried into the room beside the others and promptly cupped the frog in both hands. "Can I put Frog down now?"

"Sure. As soon as I shut the door so Hooty won't get him."

"His name's Owl," Murphy corrected as he hunkered down and set Frog on the carpet. The frog promptly took one giant hop that carried it out of sight under the bed.

"I know," Laini said, adding, "Hooty was the baby owl Glen and I found when I was your age."

"Did you keep it?"

"Until it was old enough to take care of itself, yes, we did." Memories assailed her. "Then, one summer evening, we turned it loose down at the end of the garden."

"Did its mama come for it?"

Smiling, Laini replied, "I hope so, Murphy. The next spring we heard an owl hooting, calling to another that answered from deeper in the woods. Glen and I always liked to think one of them was Hooty grown up."

Outside, Fruitful's pups were yapping up a storm that didn't sound like a squabble among themselves.

Leaving Murphy slithering under the bed to retrieve Frog, Laini started toward the front door to see what was going on. People would be calling, she realized, bracing herself. Owl, she noted with relief, was nowhere in sight.

Fruitful—what a name for a dog! she thought, amused—still lay on the top step, her tail now thumping in a friendly fashion. The puppies tumbled exuberantly around and over and under the feet of a tall, mahogany-haired man in a bulky brown, beige and white sweater, brown slacks and cowboy boots, who was striding up the walk. Watching his step, he hadn't seen her.

"Puppies!" Laini cried out, clapping her hands. "You come here—every one of you!"

As though they were accustomed to obeying her, the boisterous pack raced back along the brick walk and up the wooden steps to the porch. Immediately they launched a ferocious-sounding attack on the legs of her jeans and the laces of her sneakers.

With a grin that began at the corners of his mouth and slowly spread, the man shook his head. By the time his gaze met hers he was chuckling—a low, pleasant sound to Laini's ears—and the smile had covered his lean, deeply tanned face.

"D. J. Boone," he introduced himself, stretching out a hand although he was still several feet away from her. His voice was as deep and resonant as his laugh.

Laini smiled back. "Laini Moran." Extending her own hand, she said, "Sorry for the noisy recep—"

Under her feet a puppy yelped bloody murder. Startled, Laini missed a step and pitched forward. D.J.

leaped to catch her, only to stumble over another member of the rowdy pack.

Both Laini and he went sprawling.

Chapter Two

One thing for certain—" D.J. sounded as though he'd had the breath knocked out of him and hadn't quite gotten it back "—no one can ever say we didn't fall for each other when we first met."

Lying flat on his back on the brick walk that led to the front porch, he continued to hold her close against him in his long arms. "You all right?"

With her face buried in the curve of his neck, Laini nodded. "Yes." Her tone was so husky it surprised her. "You?"

She felt the chuckle deep in his throat—a rippling sensation against her lips—before she actually heard the low sound. "If I say I'm locked in place, will you let me go on holding you?"

Laini couldn't help laughing. "Think the puppies will let you?"

Fruitful's pups were all over both of them, their puppy barks sounding as though they'd found an exciting new trail. A cool, wet nose explored Laini's nape.

Instinctively she scrunched her shoulders and ducked her head to discourage the pup's enthusiastic snuffling, and protested, "Hey, you, stop that!" A strange excitement that had nothing to do with the puppy coursed through her.

Pushing the pups away from their faces, D.J. placed both hands at her waist and lifted her off him. A puppy promptly landed on his middle. Brushing it off, he moved with an agile grace to stand erect in what seemed like an extension of the same movement. He looked ready to burst out laughing.

Laini scrambled to her feet in a hurry. Tugging at the hem of her linen top, she dropped quickly to one knee to retie a shoelace one of the puppies had pulled loose. Her face felt ready to ignite.

What was wrong with her, anyway? she asked herself. There was no reason for her to feel so flummoxed. She had stepped on a puppy and lost her balance. D.J. had saved her from a nasty fall. That was all there was to it.

"Sure you're okay?" he asked when she was slow to straighten after she had retied the lace. Fondling the pup that was doing its best to grab the shoelace again seemed so much safer than rising and meeting his gaze.

But she took a deep breath and stood, although her knees threatened to buckle under her. Some way for a

TV reporter headed for an anchor slot on network news to react to a man, she scolded herself when a sensation of heat again raced through her, fanned by a hot wind she didn't understand at all.

"You fell hardest." The instant the words were out she could have bitten her tongue.

The warmth she'd seen in his eyes—and felt inside herself—intensified. "You're right about that," he agreed, speaking in a soft drawl that had Texas written all over it.

Attempting to ignore the impact he had on her, Laini glanced hastily around for the puppy she had stepped on. "I . . . I think I have some apologizing to do," she managed, almost casually.

Stooping, Laini scooped up a puppy and cuddled it, whispering to it. A pink tongue slurped at her chin; obviously she was forgiven.

"That dog," D.J. began, a smile in his voice as he touched the tip of an index finger to the puppy's wet black nose, "is one lucky pooch. I hope he knows that."

But there was no teasing in his eyes when Laini's gaze lifted to meet his, nor in his voice as he said gently, "Sorry about Glen, Laini."

Laini's throat closed up, as it had done in that first terrible moment when she'd heard the news. Unable to speak, she nodded, cautioning herself not to give in to the tears that lumped hot in her throat and stung her eyes.

She very nearly did, though. D.J.'s large hands closed around hers cradling the puppy. Glen would have done that, she knew. The gesture—gentle, caring, compassionate, so similar to her brother's kind of sensitivity—very nearly undid her.

"His name is Speckles," Murphy announced as he popped out onto the porch with Frog cupped in both hands and held against his T-shirt front. The screen door slammed shut behind him. "Told you last night, D.J. Me and Glen, we named 'em all."

"Sorry, Murph, I forgot." D.J.'s thumbs began to make small circles on the insides of her wrists. "Laini's got me all confused."

He was confused? Everything was a buzz in Laini's ears, although she wasn't sure whether the confusion stemmed from Murphy's presence or because D.J. had her blood racing. Had Murphy seen her lying so intimately atop D.J.?

Stop it, she chided herself. Murphy's just a little boy. Even if he did see you, he wouldn't have thought anything about it.

"Were you gonna kiss Laini, D.J.?"

Grinning, D.J. said, "No. But it seems like a smart idea."

So much for Murphy being just a little boy, Laini thought. She got her head together fast.

"I stepped on—uh—Speckles," she said, trying without much success to sound in possession of all her senses. "And Speckles forgave me."

The somber blue eyes were fixed on her face. "You wasn't kissin' D.J.?" Obviously he was disappointed.

"I wasn't kissing D.J."

Releasing the puppy into D.J.'s hands, Laini stepped quickly away from him.

Instantly she missed the warmth of his hands enveloping hers. His scent filled her nostrils and threatened her common sense, making her feel faintly giddy. What was happening to her? Had the shock of Glen's death shaken her ordered world completely apart?

D.J. gave her a teasing glance. Laini had difficulty wrenching her gaze from his. Her heart went right back into overdrive.

"Come on," she said briskly to Murphy, hoping neither he nor D.J. noticed the hint of breathlessness in her voice. "Let's put Frog in his tank while you help me get Owl into his cage.

"Then—" she risked another glance at D.J. "—maybe D.J. will help you take him down to the river as soon as it starts to get dark, and turn him loose."

Murphy regarded her with unbelieving eyes. Hugging Frog closer against his disreputable T-shirt, he asked plaintively, "Aren't you gonna come?"

"Well—" Laini hedged, trying to keep her eyes off D.J. as he leaned over and placed the puppy between Fruitful's outstretched forepaws, then scratched the old hound behind her floppy ears. "I do have to unpack. And people will be calling."

Also, she had other things to do—things, she thought with a renewed aftershock of the grief that kept rolling through her no matter how hard she tried to control it, that she didn't want to think about but must face up to.

Her father had handled everything when her mother died, and Glen had been there for her at the time of their father's death. She hadn't considered how alone she would feel when it was her turn to make funeral arrangements for someone she loved—and especially when that someone was Glen, who'd been so close to her during their growing-up years that they could have been two sides of the same coin.

How could they not have kept in closer touch, these last years? she wondered, sighing as regret assailed her once again.

Murphy's Irish-blue eyes bored into hers, touching a chord deep inside her. "Don't you think Glen'd kind of like it if you helped me and D.J. turn Owl loose, same as you helped when he let Hooty go?"

Unable to get words past the lump that suddenly was back in her throat, Laini placed an arm around the child and drew him and his frog close to her.

"That infernal bird in its cage?"

D.J., who had been seated on the back steps thinking about Glen, told Miss Annie it was, and that Laini had arrived and was unpacking.

Getting up, he held the screen door open for Miss Annie while she carried a tray covered with a red-and-white checked cloth into the kitchen. Something smelled so good it made his mouth water.

"Smells great," he told her, deciding that the Moran housekeeper was one of those women who thought food solved all sorts of problems. His grandmother out in the little Texas town near Waco where he had grown up had been like that, he remembered fondly; food on the table and a clean house, and she could cope with any emergency—except a little boy's disappointment when he was hauled back to boarding school.

"Spice cookies," the housekeeper announced, bustling over to the big square table that already held several pies and a cake fancy enough for a party. Neighbors had been bringing over food all day.

When the tray was safely set down, she lifted a corner of the checkered cloth to reveal a platter piled high with plump, rich brown cookies.

"They're still warm. Help yourself if you want some," she said, stepping back and inspecting the food with her quick glance. He could almost see her deciding whether there would be enough.

"Takes me back," D.J. said, selecting three cookies, each the size of his large palm. "My grandmother made spice cookies like these. When I was visiting she always called me when they were fresh out of the oven. I stuffed myself every time."

The housekeeper beamed. "If you run into Murphy, tell him to help himself. Not that he's apt to need telling." Her soft laugh told D.J. she liked the child. "I declare, sometimes I think that boy's empty clean down."

Thinking that she was probably right, that Murphy surely looked as if he'd missed a lot of meals in his eight years, D.J. returned to the back porch. Seating himself again on the top step, he stretched out his long legs and braced his boot heels on the old bricks that had been laid end to end in an unimaginative pattern.

The last time he'd been here, in July, he and Glen had sat out here in the dusk, watching night settle over the treetops and sift down through the branches, much as he was doing now. God, he thought, the things that could happen in a few short weeks.

If Glen had had any plan, then, to buy a plane—which, D.J. had learned, he had done a mere month later—he'd kept it to himself. D.J. frowned into the gathering dusk. It wasn't something Glen would have held back from an old friend who'd been through fire with him—not without a really good reason.

The presence of the little boy was a surprise, too, D.J. mused. According to Miss Annie, Murphy had turned up out of nowhere soon after D.J.'s return to Washington in July. Glen, she'd said, had found him scrounging food at the truck stop on the highway that bypassed Sycamore Point and had brought him home as he would have a stray puppy. Hell, D.J. thought, Glen had told him about Fruitful when she'd come straggling in, more dead than alive. He'd even asked him to shake down their acquaintances in D.C. to find someone to take a pup. So why the secrecy about Murphy?

Why the secrecy about the *plane*, for Lord's sake?

Polishing off the last of his spice cookies, D.J. put the troubling thoughts out of his mind—or tried to. Glen's secrecy just didn't track right. Glen Moran had been the most open person he'd known. More than that, it downright bugged him. He couldn't stop trying to put together reasons for it.

But Laini had to be his primary concern now, he told himself. As Glen's friend, he felt he owed it to Glen to ease her way through her grief if he could. Brushing crumbs off his thighs, he grinned in pure delight at the memory of Laini's body pressed against his. What a moment! He had felt his senses lift off, and if he was perfectly honest with himself, he wasn't sure they had yet reentered the atmosphere for an approach to reality.

Luckily, though, he mused, Laini hadn't guessed what having her on top of him had done to his libido....

"You want to go with me and Laini to turn Owl loose now?" Murphy was standing at D.J.'s elbow, although D.J. had been too caught up in fantasy about Laini to have heard the boy come outside. "Do you?" Murphy prodded.

Returning through the enchanted fog took considerable mental navigation, but D.J. managed. "Laini has things to do. Why don't you and I take him?"

"I already asked her and she's coming."

D.J. decided he was going to have to talk with Murphy and it might as well be now as later. The child needed to understand how tough these next few days were going to be for Laini, and that the two of them should give her all the support they could.

"Sit down, Murph," he invited, using the diminutive of Murphy's name he had fallen into last night.

He had seemed to like it, D.J. remembered as he indicated the top step beside him.

Murphy fidgeted from one sneakered foot to the other, but he sat, stretching his skinny bare legs out as far as they would go beside D.J.'s legs.

"Are you gonna bawl me out?" he asked warily.

"He's not going to bawl you out," Laini said as she came out onto the porch, half a cookie in one hand.

Her throaty, sensuous voice sent a ripple of excited chills skirling through his body. D.J. nearly broke a leg shooting to his feet.

Expecting Laini to laugh, or to at least smile, he swore silently at the jumpiness he felt—something he hadn't experienced since he and Glen had covered a couple of brushfire wars together. They'd been shot at from behind more rocks and bushes and buildings than he cared to recall. Once, they'd even swiped a "military" plane that Glen had piloted out of a beleaguered airstrip amid a shower of bullets.

"No, I wasn't going to bawl him out. But I just might yell at you—" the words came out a good-natured growl "—if you sneak up on me like that again. Murphy and I were just about to have a serious talk."

"Can it wait until after we turn Owl loose?" The smile he had expected hadn't even emerged as a lilt in her voice. "Someone's coming, I—" the briefest falter hinted at a nervousness barely controlled "—have to see."

"Sure," D.J. replied, sympathy welling up inside him. She and Glen might not have seen a lot of each other lately, but he knew from Glen how close they'd once been. Glen had told him Laini was all he had.

Reaching down, D.J. clapped a big hand over one of Murphy's bony shoulders. "Come on, Murph," he said in a companionable tone. "Let's go get Owl."

Then, he decided, he would take the boy somewhere for burgers and shakes while Laini made arrangements for Glen's memorial service—though he'd rather have sat beside her and held her hand; tried to take away some of the pain of her sorrow if he could.

When D.J. and Murphy returned to the back porch where Laini waited for them, Murphy carried the big gray owl in his arms, much the way he'd held Frog earlier.

A tiny smile plucked at the corners of Laini's mouth as she shook her head at the picture they made—a small boy and a huge owl at ease with each other. "And here we risked assault by beak and claw to get that bird in a carrier."

"Aw, Owl won't hurt you." Murphy's reedy voice sounded as though he meant to reassure her. "D.J. just fed him a mouse for supper. He's not hungry now."

"If you say so," she replied, wincing. After watching the round yellow eyes blink two or three times in rapid succession as the owl surveyed the wide-open dusk outside his convalescent home, Laini asked hopefully, "Why don't you release him here?"

Murphy gave her a withering glance that told her she should have known better than to make such a suggestion. "'Cause this ain't where me and Glen found him, and Glen said we oughta take him back to the same place, so he could find his way home easier."

"Oh," Laini said. *How like Glen*, she thought. She hoped it wasn't far. The man from the Drug Enforcement Administration was coming in an hour.

Frowning, she walked down the steps and waited for Murphy and D.J. to join her. Why did someone from the DEA want to talk privately with her?

Holding the owl in his arms as though he were hugging a somewhat restive feather pillow, Murphy struck off toward the woods that began at the edge of the backyard and stretched to the river several hundred feet away from the house, then north and south along the river's high bank. Laini followed the boy, and D.J., his hands shoved deep in his pockets, was at her side.

They had walked thirty or forty yards in silence when he asked, "Want to talk?"

Appreciating being given the option, Laini ran the fingers of one hand through her short black hair, which sprang right back into riotous curls. "I'd rather hear about Glen, these last few years."

She felt like a traitor. But a DEA agent was coming to question her, and she had no idea why. It made her uneasy. The only even remotely drug-related story she'd done had been the documentary on hopeless kids trapped in a homeless environment, and she couldn't imagine why it should bring a federal drug agent to her doorstep. Especially since the documentary had aired several weeks before and been given wide publicity at the time.

But Glen, during his career, had investigated drug trafficking all over the world. And drug dealers were everywhere—perhaps even here in Sycamore Point, she thought uneasily. The possibility made her shiver.

"Cold?" D.J. asked.

Laini shook her head. "Was Glen working on anything special?"

"Not that I know of." The dusk had deepened to darkness, and over their heads the tree branches laced together. She sensed his glance at her. "Except for the paper. I read the first issue this afternoon." A pause. "It's pretty great nostalgia writing."

"With Glen doing it," Laini said softly, "it would be."

They had lost sight of Murphy, but the path to the river was well defined. Feeling herself swept backward in time, she murmured, "I could walk this path blindfolded."

D.J. chuckled. "Glad to hear it. I can't see my hand in front of my face."

Involuntarily Laini reached through the darkness for his arm. When she found it she let her hand follow it downward, her palm skimming the nubby roughness of his sweater sleeve until it reached his hand, which folded around hers on contact. Her heart skipped a beat in spite of self-warnings to take it slow, which had become almost constant since she had met him that afternoon.

It was easy to push concern about the DEA agent's visit to the back of her mind—and even to forget that she wanted D.J. to tell her about Glen.

"We're almost to the old brickyard," she said, suddenly feeling the need to acquaint D.J. with her and Glen's childhood here. "One of my grandfathers built a kiln when he settled along the Wabash."

D.J. fingers meshed with hers. "Glen told me." After several steps he continued. "He also said you and he turned the ruins of the old brickworks into an imaginary fort and that each of you recruited an army to reenact the Revolutionary War as it was fought west of the Allegheny Mountains."

Despite the rush of nostalgia that saddened her, Laini laughed softly. "'Recruiting' is hardly the word. Glen recruited, I begged and cajoled. And when that failed, I threatened.

"I ended up manning the ramparts by myself half the time," she told him, smiling into the darkness. Why did talking about her childhood with Glen make her feel so much more at peace with her grief? "Being older, Glen insisted he had the right to be the hero, Colonel George Rogers Clark. That left me to pretend I was General Henry Hamilton, the British commander at Vincennes."

Chuckling, D.J. remarked, "Glen said if the British'd had you, Clark would've had a heck of a lot harder time capturing the fort."

Laini smiled again, thinking that she could almost hear her brother recounting their childhood exploits.

"Hurry up, Laini, D.J.!" Murphy pleaded from up ahead. "Owl wants to fly!"

"Then let him!"

"Let him go!"

Laini and D.J. called out in unison, and seconds later, as though homing in on their voices, the owl swooshed past their heads, a ghostly blur in the darkness.

A startled gasp caught in Laini's throat.

"Don't worry," D.J. reassured her, moving his arm around her waist. Drawing her closer against him, he added, "That's just Owl's way of saying goodbye."

"Well, he has my permission to hoot it at me from the limb of a tree!"

"Did you see him?" Murphy cried, stopping three inches short of careening into them in the darkness. "Did you see how good he flied?"

"Flew, Murphy. Did you see how well he flew?" Laini made the correction gently—in the same moment that she realized her hands had folded over D.J.'s as they spanned her waist, for all the world as though they—and hers—belonged exactly where they were.

"Did you?" Murphy repeated, oblivious to everything but Owl's accomplishment.

"Sure did, Murph," D.J. said with a chuckle. He pressed her body against his.

Laini went warm all over. It was no time to continue Murphy's grammar lesson. Or, she thought, to fuel that overactive imagination.

She wasn't sure whether she meant Murphy's imagination or her own.

Chapter Three

Can't you come, too?" Murphy pleaded, clasping Laini's fingers, which involuntarily folded around his. Moments earlier, as they walked toward the house, D.J. had mentioned taking him for burgers and shakes.

Laini gave the small hand a gentle squeeze—which wasn't at all involuntary; the boy had a way of touching her heart.

"Not tonight," she said, thinking how much she would rather accompany him and D.J. than talk with the DEA agent who was coming to see her.

"Murph," D.J. began, and stopped.

"Maybe I can go with you tomorrow," Laini promised tentatively, smiling down at the appealing, freckled face. On an impulse she said, "I'll take chocolate."

"Me too," Murphy replied, apparently satisfied.

Slipping his hand out of hers, he ran ahead of them toward the house, where the housekeeper had turned on the back-porch light.

Walking beside Laini, D.J. chuckled with a rumbly sound that teased her senses. "Why do I get the feeling you won the battle but the war's going to be a lot tougher?"

Sighing, Laini asked, "What am I going to do about him, D.J.?"

There was no way she could take Murphy with her when she left Sycamore Point after settling Glen's affairs. Her life in L.A. was hectic enough—she was away on assignment much of the time—but if she left the station for the network job, it would become even more frenetic. A young boy she hadn't known existed till that afternoon would make it next to impossible for her to give the job the absolute concentration that would be expected of her.

"I don't know." D.J. shrugged. "Find someone to adopt him, I reckon. Or let the child-welfare people place him in a foster home."

"That's easier said than done. About adoption, I mean. People want adorable infants. Newborns. Or one- or two- or three-year-olds." Why was her heart constricting the way it did every time she thought of Glen? "An eight-year-old boy and his pet frog haven't the greatest prospects for either adoption or finding a foster home." The words saddened her.

"That's a decision you'll have to make."

Glancing at him, she wondered where the tone of disapproval she heard in his voice had come from. "A lot of help you are."

"I've got decisions of my own to make."

"Oh?" she questioned, and promptly asked herself why his decisions should matter to her. After the memorial service for Glen, D.J. would go back to Washington and she wasn't apt to see him again. She might never hear from him unless it was a card at Christmas or a note when she had done a documentary he happened to see and like—or hate.

He might even have someone in his life, she mused, and couldn't believe the way her spirits plummeted at that prospect.

When he didn't speak at once, she glanced at him again, then followed his gaze. Murphy, who had fairly leaped up the four steps to the back porch, appeared frozen in midstride, like a runner caught by a fast lens, as he stared through the screen door. "D.J.," Laini whispered, stopping in her tracks, her hand going out to his arm.

Then Murphy darted back down the steps and bolted out of sight around the corner of the house.

The whole scenario lasted only a second or two.

"What the hell—" D.J.'s mutter trailed over his shoulder as he took the brick walk and the steps in strides Laini couldn't keep up with. Heart pounding, she ran up the steps behind him as he stopped short, his hand reaching out for the door.

"Virge!" D.J. sounded surprised but not alarmed.

Relieved, Laini inhaled deeply. She didn't know who was in the kitchen, but it was all right, she told herself instinctively. D.J. knew him.

Opening the screen door, he ushered her inside as a heavy-set man in a baggy seersucker suit rose from a chair pulled up to the table that, until the house-keeper had put the food away, had been piled full. A hand as large as a ham reached for D.J.'s out-stretched one.

"Virge Weiss!" D.J. grasped the man's hand. "What the heck are you doing here?"

Weiss. The DEA agent.

"Same as you," Weiss answered as they pumped each other's hands. "Saying goodbye to a friend." Fixing his gaze on Laini, he told her, "The lady that gave me this coffee and pie said to tell you she'll be back in the morning."

Nodding, Laini wished he were just paying his re-spects. She knew it might well be true—at least partly. Like any good reporter, Glen had had trusted con-tacts in all sorts of places, inside government agencies as well as in less orthodox circles. It *could* be true. But she felt uneasy.

Extending his hand to her without waiting for D.J. to introduce them, Weiss said, "Glen was a great guy, Miss Moran." He spoke in a booming, deep voice that matched his appearance. "A good friend, to me and to the agency."

"Thank you," Laini murmured, placing her hand in his and returning his firm grip. "And make it Laini, please." If you feel that way, she wanted to say, why did you sound so official when you asked to talk to me privately?

"Laini." He released her hand. "You're like Glen. Never one to stand on formality; that was Glen." As his gray eyes continued to assess her, Laini wondered if they were ever warm. "It got him in and out of a lot of places a guy like me couldn't have gone, much less come out of alive."

Never one to delay confrontation that was inevitable, she said, "You'll have to tell me about that when we have our little talk, Mr. Weiss." Although she was beginning to suspect the talk he had referred to as "little" would be far from that—at least in impact.

"Virgil." His smile was wide, but his eyes, she noted, didn't lose their frostiness. "People I'm not about to slap the cuffs on usually call me Virge."

Laini smiled but didn't make a verbal choice. Some people simply weren't cut out to make jokes, or to work undercover. Virgil Weiss she labeled as one of them. He had "hard-nosed cop" written all over him, she told herself, almost hearing and feeling the shackles snap shut on her wrists.

"Sit down and finish your pie and coffee," she suggested, indicating the huge wedge of chopped-apple pie on a plate beside his cup of coffee. "Miss Annie will never forgive you if you don't."

Taking a mug off the shelf, she poured herself coffee, then glanced questioningly at D.J. When he shook his head she added a teaspoon of nondairy creamer to her coffee and stirred it.

"Think I'll check on Murph," D.J. said. "See you later, Virge."

Nodding, Weiss sat down again and picked up his fork. He attacked the pie on his plate with the gusto of a large, hungry man who enjoyed his food and didn't worry about the consequences.

Laini sat across the table from him and took a swallow of coffee. What did he want from her?

She feared his visit had more to do with Glen than with paying his respects. Was it possible that someone Glen had investigated and then written about had sabotaged his plane? Was the DEA cooperating with the Federal Aviation Authority in investigating the cause of the crash?

It made more sense, she reflected, than her previous fear that Glen had discovered a drug connection in Sycamore Point and had been working to expose it. She hated the thought that the town she loved might have gone so sour.

"I don't bite."

Laini jumped, then realized she had finished her coffee. Weiss also had emptied both his mug and his plate. "Sorry," she said. "I was far away."

"Not so far, I'm thinking." He shook his shaggy head at her. "You couldn't be Glen Moran's sister and not be sharp as a tack."

In spite of the apprehension that had been building in her ever since his phone call, Laini responded lightly, "Why, thank you, Virgil."

"Can't make it Virge, eh?"

"Not quite yet," she answered, pushing the gnawing malaise to the back of her mind. "Maybe after we've talked."

"Fair enough," he said affably. Propping both elbows on the table, he glanced around the kitchen. Laini was certain he didn't miss a thing. "This as good a place as any?"

Nodding, she hoped he didn't suspect she had raised her guard—just a trifle. He might have been Glen's friend, but he was being too casual. If only she'd had a chance to talk with D.J. about Glen's life these past few years!

"There you are!" D.J. exclaimed easily when he finally found Murphy stretched out on his bed with Frog perched on his chest.

He had looked all over, outside, calling the child's name, blundering around the strange grounds in the dark until it was a miracle he hadn't fallen flat on his face. Fruitful's pups had frolicked around his feet, tackling first one boot and then the other, while Fruitful stretched contentedly under Murphy's window.

"Who's that man?"

Something clicked in D.J.'s mind, but he couldn't quite figure what it was. "Thought you might know him," he ventured.

Sitting up on the bed, Murphy clutched the frog closer to his chest. "Laini ain't gonna keep us, is she?"

Oh, hell, D.J. thought. So that's it. Murphy was scared witless that Virge had come to take him away, now that Glen was gone. "Maybe not," he admitted. "But don't worry about Virge. He's got seven kids of his own and four of his wife's, all under twelve." He could have added that a DEA agent's salary stretched only so far, no matter how sorry Virge might feel for a forlorn kid like Murph who wanted to be loved so badly it actually showed.

"Me and Frog—" Murphy regarded him solemnly "—we want to stay here with you and Laini."

"'Fraid you can't do that, Murph." He wished he could soften the blow but knew there was no way. And letting the child think there was a chance of him getting his wish would only make it worse. "Laini and I don't live here. We don't even live together."

Murphy's gaze didn't waver. "You could."

D.J. wiped the smile off his face before Laini turned from the doorway where she stood watching Virge Weiss pick his way down the steps through the rowdy pups. The smile had been there, he suspected, ever since Murphy had laid that crazy idea on him.

He waited until the DEA agent was in his car before he approached Laini. In the full minute or two he'd feasted his senses watching her as she stood silhouetted against the glow of the front-door light, she'd been as stiff as one of the pillars that supported the porch roof. And that had made him wonder even more what her conversation with Virge had been about.

"What'd Virge want?" he asked gently, touching her shoulder.

Still she didn't move. "You heard him. He was saying goodbye to a friend."

As his gaze followed hers across the lawn to the agent's car, D.J. muttered, "I don't buy that, and I don't think you do."

The car's headlights swept the lawn and the front of the house as Weiss backed the car and turned it around. In the glow, Laini's face appeared tense.

"Come on," D.J. said casually, "let's take Murph for those chocolate shakes and burgers."

Laini shook her head. "I can't go. Not tonight."

"Sure you can." With both hands he massaged the tight muscles in her shoulders and neck. "We'll turn out the lights and lock the door. Anyone who drops by will call again."

Again Laini shook her head. Realizing she hadn't relaxed beneath his massaging fingers, D.J. wished he had Virge Weiss's neck under his boot heel. What had the guy said to her, anyhow? He hadn't seen her this uptight since they'd met—not even when he'd told her how sorry he was about Glen and the pain in her eyes had pierced straight through to his heart.

Reluctantly he took his hands away. "Or we can go ask Miss Annie to come over and stay till we get back."

While she apparently considered that, he continued, "Murph needs you. He's scared to death Virge has come to take him away, and—"

"What gave him that idea?" Laini interrupted, turning to face him. Her eyes, meeting his, were bright with concern. His normal good sense where women were concerned had met its Waterloo. "Is that why he ran away?"

"Seems so. I found him in his room, holding Frog, and—"

"And what?" Laini prompted when he stopped short of telling her what Murph had said.

D.J. let his gaze cling to hers, searching her eyes even as he warned himself a man could drown in those eyes if he wasn't careful. How would she react if he told her about Murphy's wishful thinking about them? "I guess he was just fantasizing."

"About what?"

"You and me," he answered, trying to remember how long it had been since he'd felt about a woman as he felt now about Laini. "He wants to live here with you and me, and when I told him we don't live here, don't even live together, he simply informed me that we could."

He heard Laini's swift intake of breath, and he felt his own catch in his throat. Her smile brought relief that swept over him like a sensuous tropical breeze.

"What's that old saying about winning the battle but the war might be a lot tougher?" was her soft reply.

D.J. knew there was a grin plastered all over his face. "So what about taking Murphy out and stuffing him with burgers and fries?" Good judgment told him it was time to change the subject.

"With all that food in the kitchen?"

"I didn't see chocolate shakes in the kitchen."

Smiling, Laini said, "Good point."

Laini had won another battle, D.J. later assured her, when Murphy scurried back to his room to return Frog to the big square aquarium. Talking him out of taking the bullfrog along hadn't been easy, and she had hated doing it. Murphy was so attached to that frog it would be a sin to separate them.

What are you thinking? she demanded of herself, her heart constricting at the prospect of Murphy and Frog being separated. But it had to happen. No one would want a bullfrog in their home, even when accompanied by a beguiling, hungry-eyed child like Murphy Gonzales.

"What's wrong?" D.J. asked.

Shaking her head, Laini replied, "Nothing. I was just thinking. Murphy's probably going to have to get used to being without Frog."

"It'll break his heart."

"I know. But D.J.—" She stopped abruptly when Murphy, wearing a fresh T-shirt although he had already changed once at her request, approached, casually wiping his hands on the front of the clean shirt.

Smiling, she asked, "Ready?"

"Frog splashed me," he explained, looking at her as though he expected a reprimand for having changed shirts again. Not using the clean one as a hand towel hadn't entered his mind, she suspected.

"I'm glad you changed again," she responded.

D.J. winked at Murphy, and Laini's heart warmed. D.J. would make a wonderful father, she thought. It was too bad he was in no better a position to take Murphy than she was.

In near silence they drove in D.J.'s sports car to the truck stop Laini remembered was on the highway that bypassed Sycamore Point. She hardly recognized it. The tiny mom-and-pop operation, which had years ago consisted of a soda fountain and snack bar with two gasoline pumps, an air hose and a kerosene tank, had grown substantially. Now it included a brightly lighted restaurant, a row of attractive tourist cottages, a garage, and diesel fuel as well as more gasoline pumps. Judging from the number of cars and eighteen-wheelers in the parking area, it was a popular stop on the busy Miami-to-Chicago highway.

"How things do change," she mused aloud when D.J. had found a parking place and they were walking toward the entrance to the restaurant.

Then she thought of Glen and wished she hadn't spoken. If Weiss's suspicions were correct, this might be where Glen had made his "connection."

She didn't believe it.

Not for one minute would she think that it might be true!

Glen had hated drugs and anyone involved in the ugly traffic that trapped adults and innocent children into a habit that could surely ruin their lives. His investigative reporting proved it. Only a sincere, sensitive man could have written as he had. And if she had to, she vowed to herself, she would prove it all over again.

D.J. slowed his stride to match her lagging one. "Want to talk about it?"

"I'd like to take the rest of that apple pie and mash it in Virge Weiss's face!" Why had she spoken like that? Weiss was just doing his job.

"Go on in, Murph. We'll be along," D.J. said, obviously surprised by Laini's outburst.

Without a word Murphy dashed for the entrance, and Laini remembered that Miss Annie had said Glen had brought him here often—in fact, had found the abandoned child here at the truck-stop. *Cat's got his tongue about how he got there, though,* Annie had told Laini. *Makes a body wonder.*

It did, indeed, Laini reflected. Taking on a child—any child—was a challenge, however rewarding. Taking on one who dropped out of the blue— "Now, then," D.J. began, "let's have it. What did Virge say that upset you so?"

She told him, ending with "He didn't come straight out and accuse Glen. But he said a lot of good men succumb to the lure of the big, easy money in the drug trade, and the agency finds it hard to swallow that Glen wanted that particular plane and paid cash for it."

"What about the plane?"

Her throat tightening, she explained, "It wasn't the kind you'd expect Glen to buy. Not a small plane that someone flying for pleasure might want." Hesitating, she marshaled thoughts and emotions. "It had been used in a drug operation in the Caribbean,'' she continued, and repeated the name of the drug czar Weiss had told her was its previous owner. "Even at the auction of seized property, it sold for more money than Glen should have had lying around."

"Do I take that to mean Glen hadn't withdrawn it from his accounts?"

"I guess." Weiss hadn't come right out and said so, but she had the sick feeling in the pit of her stomach that he had known a great deal about Glen's affairs before he questioned her. Swallowing fear, she continued, "Weiss had two theories. Glen was following the drug boss's orders and buying the plane to turn over to him. Or he was in the business, had his base established here, his cover in place and was set to distribute."

"I thought," D.J. remarked dryly, "you said he didn't come right out and accuse Glen." He kicked at a plastic cup someone had discarded.

"Well, he didn't—exactly. He said there was interest in why Glen would buy a plane like that, even before the accident. I—I guess the crash precipitated things."

D.J. stopped walking and turned her to face him. Folding both her hands in his, he began to make small circles in her palms with his thumbs. "In your heart you know Glen wasn't into drugs in any way, shape or form, Laini." His voice was gentle.

"Yes. But Weiss said this place—" she looked around them at the busy truck stop "—is a natural."

Bending his head, he captured her lips in a feathery kiss. It was a mere brushing of his lips against hers, but she couldn't have spoken another word if her life had depended on it. Unable to breathe, unable to think straight, much less get words from her mind to her mouth and off her tongue, all she could think was how utterly incredible D.J. made her feel. She could take on Virgil Weiss and the whole Drug Enforcement Administration, and drug runners as well, if she had to.

"Come on," he muttered with a trace of hoarseness in his voice. "We'd better get inside before we add fuel to Murph's fantasy."

Laini managed a smile. "Would that be so bad?" she asked, and almost gasped aloud at her audacity. Never had she thrown herself at a man! Pulling away from his hand at her waist, she walked toward the entrance to the restaurant with what should have been a safe distance between them.

It wasn't.

She still sensed his nearness, and although his arm no longer circled her waist, she knew for certain he had branded her senses if not her heart. She would be a long time forgetting what D. J. Boone did to her.

But forget she must.

"What'll happen to that poor little boy now?" the middle-aged waitress asked when she brought the pot over to the table and refilled their coffee cups.

Murphy had already wolfed down two burgers and a shake and was systematically demolishing invaders from another galaxy at a game machine.

Not wanting to talk about it, Laini busied herself adding creamer to her coffee.

"Wish I knew," D.J. growled, and took a hearty gulp from his cup.

The waitress removed their plates and the empty milk-shake glasses before she continued, "I'll never forget the day Glen found him hanging 'round out front. Poor scared little kid. Took to Glen like a whipped, lost dog to a kind word."

"Glen had that effect on people," D.J. said, a trifle gruffly, and Laini could have hugged him. She had a feeling D.J. also attracted people, especially hurting people, and reached out to them wherever he went.

He took another swallow of coffee. "One thing for certain—Glen Moran won't be working off any bad karma in the next life."

"You can say that again," the waitress agreed.

"Do you have any idea how Murphy got here?" Laini asked, determined to get her mind off D.J. and how badly she wanted him to reach across the table and take her hands in his; how badly she needed him to work his special magic that seemed to flow through her when his thumbs made those small, slow circles in her palms and progressed to the pulses on the sensitive insides of her wrists.

The waitress pushed back a lock of graying dark hair. "Well, at first I thought he was from one of those trucks loaded with migrant workers that'd gone through that day. As I recall, it was at the end of July. They were tomato pickers, headed north. A lot of kids were running about while they were stopped here. It would've been easy to go off and leave one.''

Her gaze shifted to Murphy, at the video game. ''But Glen had Danny Boles go after them. He's a state cop who lives here. They said no, no one was missing. So it had to be some other way. Poor little boy...

''That's when Glen called Judge Elden and got him to get permission from the child-welfare people for him to keep Murphy till they could find out where he belonged. Way I hear it—'' the waitress interrupted herself to call out to a newly arrived couple that she would be with them right away ''—they never did, and there's not much hope they will. So Glen just kept him, and enrolled him in the local school. I heard he asked the judge to draw up adoption papers.''

Laini choked on her coffee.

When she stopped coughing, she looked over at Murphy, thinking, poor child. No wonder he seemed so bereft. His world was in shambles again, so soon after Glen had made it right by giving him hope.

Biting her lip, she watched as Murphy shoved another of the quarters D.J. had given him into the machine.

There's no way—

''Don't think about it now,'' D.J. said huskily, as though he had read her mind. Reaching across the table, he gathered both her hands in his. ''I don't know how we'll do it, but we'll work out something.''

"For Frog, too?" she whispered. The words had come so naturally, possibly because she was so shaken, so dangerously close to tears—when she hadn't wept in years.

"And Frog," he echoed, and his gaze held hers until she broke the eye contact. Then, giving her hands a squeeze, he released them. "Let's go show Murph how to really shoot down those invaders from Antares."

Making a valiant effort to clear her head—which she doubted would happen very quickly or stay that way for long where D.J. was concerned—she asked, "Is that where they're from?"

How could a man she'd just met cast such a spell on her senses? She felt as though she had known him always—and wanted him in her life forever.

Chapter Four

Crisp, sweet air drifting across her face, its touch as soft and gentle as a lover's caress, wakened Laini.

Beyond the open window beside her bed was darkness black as black velvet, not the security-lighted pale brilliance that from dusk to dawn spilled through the apartment complex in Los Angeles where she lived.

Not a mutter of traffic broke the quiet; not a single siren wailed within her hearing. The only noise she heard was a low cry of a night bird, off toward the river. With a contented sigh she turned over in bed and settled herself again.

How wonderful to be home!

Then she remembered Glen.

A pain stabbed through her. As she sat up in the bed she hadn't slept in for so many years, she realized what had wakened her. And it hadn't been the sweet, crisp air touching her skin with such sensuousness that she felt loved. It had been the chilling fog she now felt spreading through her.

What was she going to do?

The property presented no problem. If she couldn't bring herself to part with it at once, she could let Miss Annie and her husband and Judge Elden look after it as they'd done since her father's death. Someday... maybe, *someday* ... she might want to do as Glen had done: come home.

But what about Murphy?

She wanted a child, maybe two, someday. But that was in the future... when she'd met that special man. So, she mused, why was she considering tying herself down, now, with an eight-year-old straight out of *Huckleberry Finn*—no matter if he had melted her heart with those amazing blue eyes?

Stop it, Laini. You're not Glen. A now familiar pang of remorse shot through her as she thought how alike they once had been, and yet how different. Glen had made his mark in the world and then come home. She was still chasing her dream. She didn't have time to stop until she had attained her goal.

But could she find the time? Flopping over in bed, she pounded the pillow as though her sleeplessness were the pillow's fault. People could always make time for something they wanted badly enough, couldn't they? Besides, wasn't it time she had something other than her career?

The question stung. The salt of reality rubbed into the wounds left by hot pursuit of her goal, she thought, reminded of a few things she'd just as soon forget and of prospects she'd rather not think about. The time would come—for her as it had for others—when studio and network brass would decide they wanted a younger woman, a fresh, new image, in front of their cameras, and she would be forced into production or management. Or even retirement.

What would she do then? Wish futilely that she had changed her life when she'd had the chance? Wish she had children who would have given her grandchildren to love and to nurture?

"Oh, Laini," she wailed aloud in a whisper that was almost a whimper, "you've really gotten yourself on a downhill slide this time!"

Pulling on a faded terry robe, she wondered where the depression had come from. She usually didn't beat herself over the head. She'd seldom doubted she would make it big and be happy all the way—not even when the one or two truly best friends she'd made over the years had tried to warn her of the time when she might decide her climb toward success would seem not worth the cost to her personal life. She hadn't believed them, hadn't heeded her own infrequent doubts.

So why, now, were her heart and her mind playing tricks on her? Why did moving to the network—the logical next step she had planned for so long and which appeared within her reach at last—suddenly seem less important than it had up to this point?

"I can't believe what I'm thinking!" she muttered into the darkness as she let herself into the hall and eased the bedroom door shut behind her. *She*, come home as Glen had done and give Murphy a home and the love he appeared so starved for? The love and affection she knew she could shower on a child?

Give up everything she had worked so hard to achieve?

Laini Moran, that's crazy! *You* would be crazy to even consider it!

As soon as she cleared Glen's name, she thought, she would be off, would get on with her own life....

Around her was silence, except for the whisper of the wind in the leaves of the huge sycamore trees that surrounded the house; leaves already turned parchmentlike and beginning to fall. D.J., in the room next to hers, must be sleeping like a log, she thought enviously. She didn't hear a sound from there. Across the hall, Murphy undoubtedly was sleeping the sleep of a small active boy who had devoured burgers and shakes and defeated invaders on video screens until she and D.J. had almost literally dragged him home.

Moving quietly along the hall, she relished the familiar feel of the thick carpet under her bare feet. Never had she felt further from sleep, yet she knew she needed the rest. The next few days were certain to be emotionally and physically exhausting. Already she felt the strain. That insane idea about her returning permanently to Sycamore Point and adopting Murphy was proof.

"Warm milk," she murmured, "and then back to bed with you, Laini Moran, to get your head together."

Sighing, she wondered if warm milk would do it. The DEA agent's suspicions about Glen lay heavily on her mind. What, exactly, hadn't she liked about Weiss? she wondered as her hand went unerringly to the light switch inside the kitchen.

"You can't sleep either, huh?"

Surprised, Laini blinked owlishly at D.J.

"You look like you can use my grandmother's remedy for sleepless nights." D.J. shut the back door where he'd been standing looking out when she flipped the light on. His glance swept over her, warming her as it traveled. "She used to say a glass of warm milk would quiet anybody's skittery nerves."

"My nerves aren't skittery," she lied. They were— now. D.J. wore the brown slacks he'd had on earlier and leather slippers but no shirt. The mahogany hair that curled on his chest was a definite hazard to her senses. She tore her gaze away and forced her eyes to meet his.

"You could have fooled me."

Feeling her color rising, Laini cautioned herself to watch it. She had been warming milk alone in the middle of the night for years. Now, when she felt especially vulnerable, was the worst possible time to let herself think how nice it was to share that intimacy with a man—no, she corrected her musing, not *a* man, not just any man—*D.J.*

"I'll get the pan," she said, stooping quickly to rummage beneath the counter. "You get the milk from the fridge."

When she straightened, an enamel saucepan in one hand, he was so close to her she suddenly couldn't breathe.

"You look mighty fetching."

Willing herself, Laini took the milk container from him, making the mistake of letting her hand brush lightly against his. Electricity jolted through her.

"This robe didn't make me look fetching when Glen gave it to me." Oh, God. Why had she said that? She might sound in control, but she felt shaken by the memory of that last "family" Christmas. And why did she feel compelled to explain to him? "It . . . was the last Christmas all of us had together. Before . . . Mother died."

Placing the saucepan on the burner, she poured in the milk and turned the burner to low heat before she handed the container back to him, being careful, this time, not to touch his hand with her own.

"Good memories can be rough, times like these," he said gently as he returned the milk to the fridge.

Feeling all teary inside, she whispered, "Yes. They can."

"Whatcha making?" Murphy, who'd suddenly appeared in the doorway, sounded as though he hadn't wolfed down two burgers and a large shake only a few hours before.

Laini exhaled the breath she'd held so she wouldn't cry. "Warm milk."

"Can I have some?"

"Of course you may!" she exclaimed, her heart going out to him again. Poor little boy. He sounded so lost and alone—and so fearful. Just the way she felt.

"Sure thing, Murph." D.J. spoke in unison with Laini. "What's the matter? Can't sleep?"

Murphy's glance darted back and forth between them. Slowly he shook his head.

Winking, D.J. said, "Seems to be a lot of that going 'round. Don't worry about it."

Laini concentrated on stirring the warming milk. Murphy definitely suspected he had interrupted something. She didn't know whether to be amused or irked.

"Me and Frog...was scared."

The plaintive young voice struck straight to Laini's heart. Before she was aware of having moved, she dropped the wooden spoon she'd been using to stir the milk and was on her knees in front of him. He clutched Frog to his scrawny bare chest as though he thought the frog was his last friend in all the world and feared that, if he let go, he would lose it, too.

"Oh, Murphy," she whispered, gathering him close, "you and Frog don't have to be afraid!"

Murphy drew back so he could peer into her face. "D.J. said—"

"What does D.J. know?" Laini demanded, looking at D.J. across the boy's tousled hair. She hugged him so tightly Frog squirmed between them. "You and Frog don't have to worry! D.J. and I will see to that."

What had she just said?

Giving Murphy another hug, she continued huskily, "Now then. Can you put Frog down, wash your hands and get the cups for me?"

"One for D.J., too?"

"One for D.J., too," Laini echoed as she stood up, her blood suddenly thundering in her ears. She didn't dare glance at D.J.

"Well, now—" D.J. began when Murphy had finished his warm milk in record time and, after retrieving Frog from under the table, returned to his room "—it's sure going to be interesting to see how you get out of that."

With a teasing glance at her, he rocked the sturdy, ladder-backed chair on its back legs and balanced it there.

Laini felt as though her face were primrose pink. How could she, even in the rush of compassion for Murphy, have forgotten what he'd said to D.J.? She and D.J. together? Not even for Murphy! Not even if he did make her insides feel quivery and magical, as no man had made her feel before.

Fleeing the fantastical sensations before they made her forget all about anchoring the network news in New York, she said, "You know what I mean."

D.J. reached for his mug and very nearly spilled the milk onto the floor and himself from his precarious perch. "*I* know what you mean," he replied, righting himself. He very nearly flung the words at her: "But I wonder if Murphy does."

Laini swallowed cooling milk that suddenly was
tasteless in her mouth. Murphy probably had gone
back to bed with visions of a life here with her and
D.J. come true—his little-boy dream, however un-
realistic, magically realized. She should say something, she knew, but she couldn't find words.

"Hell, Laini—" D.J. wasn't quite scowling at her
"—you saw him. He perked right up." The chair tee-
tered perilously again before its front legs cracked on
the floor. "It's likely he's the only one of the three of
us who'll get any sleep the rest of the night."

She wouldn't sleep, that was for sure. "I always
suspected hot milk was a myth."

His gaze warming, he said teasingly, "There's always sex. The great relaxer."

"And conversation," Laini countered, then corrected herself: "*Or* conversation." She smiled when he
grimaced comically. "Tell me about Glen."

She expected some bantering remark about disap-
pointing Murphy. But D.J. was all business as he
leaned forward, folding his bare arms on the table. His
gaze locked on to hers. Laini had a little trouble with
her breathing until she managed to corral the desire
that had begun to stir within her.

"Glen wasn't into drugs," she began, willing herself to ignore the warmth that suffused her body in
spite of her resolve. "I know that in my soul."

"So do I." D.J. nearly blew her already shaken re-
straint by reaching across the table and folding both
her hands in his. "Don't be too hard on Virge. He's a
good agent. He's going to follow every lead he can

come up with and knock himself out giving Glen a clean bill.''

"Then why did he insinuate all those terrible things? He sounded as though he thinks Glen finally crawled out from under the slimy rock he'd been hiding under all these years.'' She didn't like to think that Weiss had made some good points. Why *did* Glen bid on that particular plane, and pay for it with cash that hadn't come from any bank account Weiss had been able to find?

D.J.'s hands tightened momentarily around hers, as though he'd read her thoughts. "That's just Virge's way," he said quietly, "He's lost a lot of friends the hard way in the fifteen or twenty years he's been with the agency.''

Laini had no response to that; she realized it could well be true. Fighting drug traffic, even writing about it—sometimes going undercover as Weiss had told her Glen had done—was a dangerous business.

"How could he have paid Glen such glowing tribute," she said, remembering her conversation with the agent, "and in the next breath pointed a finger at him, the way he did?''

After silent moments D.J. released her hands and ran long fingers through his hair. Something was very wrong, she thought, a quiver of dread running through her even before he said, "I think you'd better tell me everything Virge said. And I mean everything, Laini.''

Laini inhaled deeply. To her, *everything* included her gut reaction to Weiss's manner as well as his words—the instincts that screamed in her mind for utterance. "Do you trust him?" she asked quietly.

"I never had any reason not to." D.J. was laconic. "And I've known him a long time." He seemed to be searching for something. "We met a year or two before I met Glen, although I haven't seen him often. I'd say Glen knew him better than I do."

A scowl knitting his thick brows, he continued. "I always thought Virge leaked information to Glen. Glen likely returned the favor when he could do it without betraying a source. Glen was a bear about protecting sources."

Throat aching, Laini nodded her agreement. Unshed tears stung her eyes and nearly spilled over when D.J.'s hands moved across the table to cover hers, clasped tightly on the table in front of her.

"We don't have to talk about this tonight," he said gently. "You've had a hard day, and tomorrow will be worse."

"*Today* will be worse." Laini released a quavery breath. She managed a faint smile as her eyes met his. "Do you know what time it is?"

It was very nearly dawn—the darkest hour of the darkest day of her life. Thank heaven D.J. was here.

Standing, D.J. reached for the milk mug she had emptied and the one Murphy had used and carried them and his own to the sink, where he rinsed them and the saucepan and then placed them in the dishwasher while she watched. After drying his hands on a paper towel, he turned to her.

"Now, then," he announced, with a ghost of the smile she'd found mesmerizing, "I'm going to tuck you in."

Laini smiled in spite of herself.

"D.J.?" The hammering on his bedroom door became louder. "D.J.?"

What an alarm clock! D.J. thought. He'd wake Laini for sure. Rolling out of bed and reaching for his pants in the same motion, he growled, "Coming, Murph."

He opened the door just as Murphy raised small fists to pound again. "Hold it down, Murph. You'll wake Laini."

"I just looked in. She's sleeping."

"After you knocked?"

"Didn't knock."

D.J. pulled him—and Frog, in its usual perch, held against Murphy's middle—into the room.

Shutting the door, he grumbled, "You shouldn't go peeping into Laini's bedroom without knocking."

Murphy fidgeted from one sneakered foot to the other. "Didn't hurt nothing. I just wanted to see if you was still—if you—"

"What the heck gave you that idea?"

Squirming, Murphy began, "I watched you—"

When he broke off again, D.J. tousled his already tousled hair, thinking, nosy kid. "It's all right, Murph. Just don't go around spying on your friends. Or anyone else, for that matter. It'll get you in trouble."

"Okay." Murphy accepted the advice with what D.J. privately labeled water-off-a-duck's-back insouciance.

Then the boy asked expectantly, "Did you kiss her?"

Keeping his face straight with an effort, D.J. replied, "As a matter of fact, no, I didn't."

Murphy's face didn't fall, it crashed. "Why didn't you? Laini said—"

D.J. gave him a man-to-man poke in the shoulder. "Why don't you go see if the morning paper has come, while I shave and shower. Then we'll have breakfast and talk about it."

He had no idea what he would say to Murphy later, but he didn't want to face the child's precociousness now. After shooing Murphy out, he unzipped his suitcase and got out his razor, shaving cream and after-shave, and fresh clothing, and headed for the bathroom.

It was going to be an interesting several days....

Laini winced at the sight of Frog seated at Murphy's elbow on the dining-room table, but since Miss Annie, who was refilling D.J.'s coffee cup, apparently hadn't objected, she didn't protest, either. Glen, she thought, must have run a very loose ship.

"Good morning, all," she said cheerfully.

D.J.'s gaze said all sorts of things to her over the top of the newspaper he was reading; his "Morning, Laini" made her think of last night.

She had been a long time getting to sleep.

"Another newsaholic, I see," she commented lightly, when he went back behind the morning *Evansville Courier*.

"Hard habit to break." Folding the newspaper, D.J. laid it beside his place.

"Tell me about it," she said wryly, smiling. The children of newspaper parents, she and Glen had learned to read from newspapers before they went to kindergarten; their days from breakfast on had been filled with the printed page in one form or another. "Glen and I had the morning paper every day with our oatmeal and orange juice, the afternoon editions with our dinner. In between we read everything else we could get our hands on."

She was talking too much, she scolded herself. Conscious of D.J.'s and Murphy's eyes following her every move, she placed crisp bacon, jelly and toast on her plate and carried it from the buffet back to her place at the long dining table. Miss Annie already had poured her coffee.

Smiling across the table at Murphy, she remarked, "I feel guilty eating in front of Frog. Why don't you put him in the aquarium until we finish? Then you can feed him."

"Will you help me?"

"Sure," Laini promised, and Murphy was off like a shot.

D.J. chuckled. "You asked for it. Know what a frog eats?"

"Of course I do. I'm Glen's sister, remember?"

The words left her feeling sad, but the memories they evoked were good. She and Glen had had good times in this house, in the woods that stretched along the river, and many of them had included wildlife. Even bullfrogs whose resonant *chug-a-rumm*ing on warm summer nights had been something to hear— and remember when she'd been lonely and missing home.

Murphy came galloping back, and as they ate, he chattered on about Frog and Owl. Laini couldn't help thinking they were almost a family—not three strangers who had been brought together by the death of a man each of them had loved in his or her own way.

What if it did happen? What if she and D.J. . . . ?

Don't, Laini, she cautioned herself. Don't set yourself up for heartbreak.

Chapter Five

Laini tensed when the doorbell rang. On her second cup of coffee, she still wasn't ready to hear how sorry someone felt about Glen. To be honest, she admitted to herself, she hadn't realized yet this morning how bleak her own world was without him.

She'd wakened mesmerized by memories of last night. D.J.'s walking her to her bedroom had stirred sensations that her better judgment had warned, futilely, she would be better off without.

His long, bare arm around her shoulders had threatened to scorch her flesh right through the thick terry-cloth robe and the oversize T-shirt she wore for sleeping.

She'd scarcely been able to breathe when he removed the robe and, gathering her in his arms, lifted her to the middle of the double bed and laid her back against the pillows. Although such a rushing into things was against every value she'd set for herself and, thus far, had maintained, she had wanted more than anything for him to come after her.

But all he'd done was pull the quilt over her and, after an almost imperceptible pause and a tremor scarcely visible in his hands, on up to cover her trembling body all the way to her chin.

With a beguiling smile that had set a flock of butterflies loose inside her, he'd turned off the bedside lamp he had flipped on with his elbow as they'd entered the bedroom, and left.

Remembering, she managed not to sigh aloud.

Breakfast hadn't been much better. She'd been swept up, like Dorothy and Toto in a Kansas tornado, in a sweet fantasy of how it might be for D.J. and her—for D.J., Murphy and her—if she were to let the emotions that churned inside her have their way; if she—and D.J.—were to let Murphy's yearning to make them his family actually happen.

It might, if she wasn't careful, she thought. She could fall in love with D.J.; she felt halfway in love with him already, she admitted musingly to herself as the doorbell rang again and Miss Annie padded briskly along the hall to answer it.

Already she felt a burst of warmth every time D.J. touched her, and she nearly drowned in his eyes every time their glances met.

But she mustn't let it happen. Falling in love would be a disaster.

With an inaudible sigh, she realized she couldn't define all the feelings that drenched her. The passion, she understood; she'd felt it before, although never quite like this, she thought. It had never been something she wasn't sure she could handle.

How did she deal with feeling safe and warm, old-shoe comfortable? With a man she'd only just met?

"Murph—" D.J.'s deep, faintly gravelly voice brought her back "—why don't you and I go give Frog his breakfast while Laini talks with whoever's at the door?"

Murphy's gaze leaped to her face, then to D.J.'s. "Laini said she wants to help me feed him."

"She does want to." D.J., she thought, sounded as though he'd dealt with small boys before.

"I'll help you next time, Murphy," Laini promised.

"Sure she will, Murph. Right now, she's got other things to do. You and I need to help her all we can."

Murphy looked down at his plate, gleaned off the last smidgen of the bacon and scrambled eggs the housekeeper had kept heaping on it during the meal. "What do you want me to do?"

"We'll talk about it while we feed Frog," D.J. replied gently. He pushed back from the table, and Murphy slid sideways out of his chair. "If you need us, Laini," D.J. said, "give a shout."

Laini nodded and watched him until he disappeared into the kitchen, following Murphy's darting figure. He took with him whatever pleasantness she'd found in the morning.

A little later, Laini stared at the letter Judge Elden had brought her.

Her adopt Murphy?

Raise him in Sycamore Point?

She couldn't believe Glen could even have dreamed of making such impossible requests. But there they were, in Glen's familiar, practically illegible scrawl.

"When did you get this?" she asked the judge in a whisper.

The judge looked at her in obvious sympathy. "Glen hand-delivered it a few hours before he left for Atlanta. He said he was driving to Evansville, where he had left the plane."

Laini moistened her lips. "Do you . . . think he had a premonition of some sort?" She didn't believe in omens, but why else would Glen have left such a letter?

The judge took his glasses off and massaged the narrow bridge of his nose.

"Glen was a practical man, Laini. He knew the risks—he always had." He heaved a sigh. "This isn't the first letter I've held for you when he felt his life might be in danger. Prior to this, I've been fortunate enough to have been able to destroy them unread."

"Did he tell you why he felt he was in danger this time?"

Holding her breath, Laini focused on the envelope with *Laini* written across it as she waited for his answer.

"No." The answer came slowly, the single syllable drawn out in the fine old voice that once had resonated through southern Indiana courtrooms, often while Laini and Glen had listened. The judge had been one of their favorite people. "He never did, though I knew it was a very real danger he would be facing. Each time I shook his hand, I feared it might be the last."

Chewing her bottom lip to stop its sudden trembling, Laini read the last two paragraphs of the letter again, and decided that Glen had suspected these might, indeed, be his last words to her.

In the event of my death, I hope you, Laini, will adopt Murphy Gonzales, as I intended to do as soon as Judge Elden could get his past untangled, and that you will raise him in Sycamore Point with all the love and sense of family you and I knew during our childhood.

Love you, Laini.

Glen's signature spilled off the bottom of the page, as though he'd been in a great hurry to get on with whatever venture it had been that had led to his death on that mountain.

"I love you too, Glen," she echoed softly.

She'd never felt closer to him—but, she thought, there was no way she could do as he requested. Although she might adopt Murphy, raising him in Sycamore Point was out of the question.

No matter how wonderful a life it could be.

* * *

"You look green around the gills, Mr. Boone," the housekeeper observed with a twinkle, some time later, when she met him and Murphy in the hall outside Murphy's room.

They had just finished feeding Frog and were headed for the old brickworks on the river where, Murphy had confided, "Glen used to take me a lot."

Grimacing, D.J. asked, "Have you ever fed chopped liver, earthworms and lettuce to a bullfrog right after eating your own breakfast?" His stomach still felt queasy.

The housekeeper's eyes danced behind her glasses. "Aren't you the same young man I heard teasing Laini at the breakfast table about what a frog eats?"

He laughed and figured it was time to change the subject. "Who's that with Laini?" Although he and Murphy had been a while with Frog, the murmur of voices still came from the dining room. Laini and someone were having quite a conversation.

"Judge Elden." Her tone told him how much she liked, respected and trusted the judge. "Timothy's been a family friend since before Glen and Laini were born. Harley and I both went to school with him and Glen, Senior. He's always handled legal matters for the family."

D.J. didn't know how he could feel so much better than he had, mere moments earlier. Even his stomach settled perceptibly.

"Can I let Speckles out to come with us?" Murphy yelled over his shoulder as he shot out the back door, causing Fruitful's puppies, in the kennel out back, to go wild.

D.J. caught the door before it banged. "I don't see why not."

At Miss Annie's suggestion, the dogs—which, D.J. suspected, virtually lived on the front porch where they could have first crack at welcoming anyone who set foot in the Moran yard—had been penned in the spacious run Glen had built for them, and then, according to the housekeeper, rarely used.

"Let's take them all," he called out in a sudden burst of warmth that rushed through him. He owed those pups, especially Speckles. If they hadn't been underfoot, he would have missed those few moments of intimacy with Laini. Thinking about it had kept him warm all night.

"Fruitful, too?"

"Fruitful, too," he echoed, grinning to himself at the name the housekeeper had said Glen hung on the old hound after she presented him with the seven pups two days after he took her in. "We'll have to put them all back in the pen, though. You heard Miss Annie. Can't have them jumping all over people when they come to call."

He doubted Murphy heard a word he uttered after "take them all."

The boy raced down the porch steps and across the yard, his sneakered feet whipping through tall grass that Harley Bensinger had "considered" mowing, then decided not to because "Glen wanted it to seed itself and be winter cover and food for field mice and rabbits.

"Then," Harley had continued, "there's a vixen down there in the woods somewhere that's always brought her kits out in the spring to catch mice. Glen liked to watch them. She may be back, and I'd like to show the boy."

"Glen would like that," D.J. had said, feeling touched.

Now, with the same pang stabbing through him, he sensed that reminders of Glen Moran were everywhere.

What would happen now? To Murphy? Frog? The dogs?

And to the old house Glen had called a part of himself and of Laini?

Think about it, Boone. If you're ever going to take a chance on that book that's in your head, now's the time to do it—while you're young enough to go back working for someone else if you fall flat on your face.

Thinking that he could use another cup of coffee he stepped up his pace until he was in sight of Murphy and the pups.

Murphy, on his knees, egged the pups on as they scratched and dug and *woof*ed around a rotting stump. As he watched, Fruitful ambled over to investigate but abandoned the search after a couple of tentative sniffs, then flopped down to watch in comfort.

"That's what I say, old girl." D.J. hunkered beside her. Scratching the soft places behind her floppy ears, he said congenially, "Let the kids have their fun."

Laini didn't know what she was missing, he mused. Murphy was having a ball. The kind of fun a kid who felt secure in the embrace of a family enjoyed.

How the hell, he wondered, could she have set him up for a letdown, the way she had, last night?

You and Frog don't have to worry.

He could still hear her.

Sure, she'd spoken on impulse. Sure, she meant to find a home for him, the same as she would for Fruitful and the pups.

But it was still going to tear the child apart when he found out she hadn't meant *she* would keep him, the way Murphy had said Glen had intended to keep him: "For forever."

When the judge had gone, Laini didn't need Miss Annie to tell her D.J. and Murphy had gone down to the river and had taken Fruitful and the pups with them.

The minute she stepped out of the kitchen onto the porch she heard the puppies' high-pitched, exuberant barks—already hinting at the throaty baying-hound voices they would develop as they grew older—and Murphy's equally gleeful shouts.

What was she going to do *now*? she asked herself as she let herself be drawn toward the happy sounds as though she expected to find the answers to her question down by the river.

"Oh, Glen," she murmured aloud, "how could you?"

Taking Murphy to her heart was one thing. He was already there and had been from the moment she'd laid eyes on him, melting her common sense until she sometimes wondered if she could walk away from him when the time came that she must return to Los Angeles—and then move on to the new job in New York.

If she didn't grab the opportunity, she stood to lose the best chance she was apt to encounter to make it really big.

The adoption she could handle, although it wouldn't be easy for either her or for Murphy. She wasn't even sure it would be fair to Murphy. For all the love and affection she could give him when they were together, if her career continued at the same frenzied pace it had the past few years—and she had every reason to believe it would—she would be with him rarely.

Rearing him in Sycamore Point was something else.

Much as she'd enjoyed her own childhood in the small town, Glen had had no right to expect her to give up the life she had made for herself. For her, it might be now or never.

The realization hit her like a ton of bricks.

D.J. sat on a remnant of wall that had been part of a kiln in which her ancestors had burned bricks. His gaze was focused off across the river, while Murphy and the pups romped through the ruins of the small, tumbled-in building that she and Glen had pretended was the Revolutionary War-time Fort Sackville, at nearby Vincennes. Neither Murphy nor D.J. saw her coming.

Before nostalgia got the best of her, Laini stepped close to D.J. and slipped her arms around his waist. Immediately an explosion rocked her senses—and, apparently, his. He caught her hands before she could withdraw them in surprise.

"Don't," he said hoarsely, his hands folding around hers. "I need them there."

"So do I," she whispered honestly, trying to understand how she could feel as she did about a man she'd met only a short time ago.

Neither of them spoke for a couple of moments; neither of them moved. Laini wondered what he was thinking; if he was as aware of her as she was of him; if Murphy's happy shouts and the puppies' rambunctious yapping sounded as far away to his ears as they did to hers.

She wondered if Glen knew the havoc his death had turned loose in her life.

Oh, God, she thought. Where had *that* come from?

Glen had never wanted anything but the best for her. And he wouldn't, now.

But to give up everything she'd worked so hard to achieve and return to Sycamore Point? For vacations, maybe—but she'd never even done that.

She lifted her cheek from its sweet repose against D.J.'s shoulder. "You'll never guess what Judge Elden just told me."

What Glen just told me. Oh, heaven, she thought. Why did she feel as though she'd heard Glen's voice instead of read his scrawled handwriting?

"This whole mess is a bad dream?"

His hands tightening on hers, he turned his head. Instantly a breath hung up in her throat. The hurt in his eyes, on his compressed lips, was so visible she wanted to kiss it away.

"Don't I wish," she whispered, her voice suddenly husky, her throat aching.

If only it were a bad dream!

If only she could wake up and find it was all part of another of Glen's resourceful schemes to go undercover without arousing suspicion! How she would enjoy rubbing Virgil Weiss's nose in that!

Murphy and the pups raced past them, boy and dogs in full cry as though they chased imaginary game through an imaginary forest.

Laini scarcely heard them. Without speaking, D.J. had drawn her between his knees and his arms had gone around her waist. Although it was a loose embrace—the embrace of one friend comforting another, she tried telling herself—she felt bewitched.

Snatching at reality before it eluded her totally, she blurted out, "Glen wants me to stay in Sycamore Point and raise Murphy."

The beguiling, lopsided grin that never failed to shake her senses began at one corner of his mouth. "Sounds good to me."

"I can't do it. I don't dare even consider it. I've worked too hard for too long to get where I am." She took a deep breath. "Adoption, maybe. But—"

"Whoaaa."

Interrupting, D.J. took his hands away from the now thoroughly sensitized small of her back, leaving behind myriad warm sensations that skittered about in total disarray.

"What about adoption?"

Inhaling deeply, Laini began at the beginning. "A few hours before he left for Atlanta, Glen took a letter for me to Judge Elden. He was going to adopt Murphy, but in the...event of his death—" she had trouble with the phrase "—he wanted me to adopt Murphy and raise him here in Sycamore Point." She recited the part about the love and sense of family she and Glen had known in their childhood. Then, dragging a breath deep to give her strength, she said, "The adoption, I can handle."

"How?" The soft, west Texas drawl that always did such devastating things to her insides had gone hard. "What'll you do, Laini?" he demanded, still holding her but as though she were a stranger. "Enroll him in a private school where he'll stick out like a sore thumb among kids who've had every advantage to his none, while you go on clawing your way to the top?" He snorted angrily. "I went that route. My father left when my mother decided her precious career meant more to her than he did. The next few years I bounced in and out of more fancy schools than I can count."

He swore under his breath. "Murphy deserves better."

"What do you expect me to do?" Laini snapped.

"If this wasn't official business—" Virgil Weiss's rumbly, wheezy voice shattered the angry silence that followed her outburst "—I'd go back and let you fight it out. But I don't have the time. If I'd had more time

I wouldn't be walking all over looking for you. I'd have waited in the car. Miss Annie told me you were down here.''

"What's up, Virge?" D.J. growled.

"Couple of things."

For a long moment, Weiss stared off across the river, his gaze seeming tangled in willows that sprouted at the water's edge and ranged up the bank to the band of sycamores that rimmed the river up- and downstream.

Something was on his mind, for sure, Laini thought, bracing herself.

Turning to face her, Weiss said, "First, the bad news. I need to look around Glen's room, Laini."

"And the good?" she asked, keeping her voice level with an effort when her insides began to quiver.

"Don't get your hopes up, but a backpacker thought he saw a parachute just before Glen's plane hit that mountain and exploded."

Laini's heart leaped. "Are you saying Glen may be alive?"

"I'm saying don't get your hopes up—" Weiss cleared his throat "—but don't give up hope."

"You're not making much sense, Virge."

D.J., Laini reflected, sounded as though something were stuck in his throat and he wasn't sure what it was. She felt the same way.

"You should know by now if Glen was in that plane when it hit or he wasn't," D.J. pointed out.

The DEA agent shoved his big hands into his coat pockets and looked even more uncomfortable than he

had last night as he'd talked with her about Glen
maybe being a drug ring's "Sycamore Point connection."

What was going on? she wondered. Virgil didn't
strike her as an empathetic man. For all that he'd been
Glen's friend, why had he gone out of his way to tell
her not to get her hopes up but not to give up hope,
either?

He wasn't being kind, whether he realized it or not.
They both knew Glen was dead. No one could walk
away from a plane that had exploded on impact, the
way Glen's had. Why couldn't Virge just go away and
leave her alone with the grief she'd begun more or less
to come to grips with?

If Glen had parachuted from the plane, he would
have been in touch with her the minute his feet hit the
ground. No way would he have broken her heart, and
Murphy's, by letting them think he was dead.

"Wish I could make sense out of Glen Moran being
involved in the traffic," Weiss muttered, fixing his
mist-gray eyes on them both. Laini couldn't help
shivering.

He spun around and headed for the house, words
trailing over his shoulder. "Wish I could tell you he
wasn't."

Chapter Six

Across the hall from her own, Glen's room was almost exactly as it had been before he'd left home to go to college. There were more books, of course; and the mementos he'd brought home from faraway places. A personal computer now stood beside Glen's electric typewriter and the ancient manual machine their father had used in his own newspaper work. But essentially it was the same: a boy's room grown into a man's room, reflecting his personality and interests.

Laini's eyes swept over everything, following Weiss's searching gaze.

What was he looking for? she wondered. Even if his suspicion was valid, did he think Glen would have been stupid enough to leave anything incriminating lying around for Miss Annie to see when she did her regular cleaning? Or for Murphy to stumble across and start asking questions about?

When Weiss turned on the computer's power switch and punched keys that brought copy to the screen, she glanced at D.J.

Standing beside her, he jammed his fists deeper into his pockets. Lifting mahogany brows would have answered her unspoken question if the clenched fists hadn't; D.J., she decided, was as provoked as she by Weiss's incredible charges. He seemed to have forgotten his irritation with her over what to do about Murphy.

"If you'll tell me what you're looking for," she began, trying to keep her cool as Weiss peered at the computer screen, "maybe I can help you."

Fat chance. What she'd like to do was tar and feather the man. When she'd caught up with him on the path from the river and asked if he knew something he hadn't told her, he'd just about snapped her head off.

Weiss scanned the list of entries on the computer disk, seeming to hesitate over one or two, before he punched off the power and returned to examining the room.

"I don't know what I'm looking for," he admitted finally. "Something to get me off your hit list, I suppose, but that's not what I'm here for."

"Laini understands that, Virge." D.J.'s voice was hard as nails.

"*I* thought you were Glen's friend," Laini said, "and that friends trusted each other."

Catching the inside of her bottom lip between her teeth, she wondered how she could think, however obliquely, that Virgil must think he had probable cause to suspect Glen, or he wouldn't be here—tip or no tip. Had Glen changed so much in the years they'd been apart?

Dragging a breath deep into her lungs, she added coolly, "I'm going to have to ask you to wait until after the memorial service to continue your search, Virgil. Glen's friends, his *real* friends, and neighbors will be in and out of the house. Several will be staying overnight. I'd rather they not know your suspicions until they have to—*if* they have to."

She gave him a level look that told him candidly what she thought of him and his accusations. "And bring a warrant when you come."

"Sorry you feel that way, Laini." Shaking his head as though her stand saddened him, he broke eye contact and turned to D.J. "See you, Deej."

D.J. folded a big hand over the top of Laini's shoulder and gave her a comforting squeeze before he followed Weiss from the room.

When he returned several minutes later, she was leafing through the well-worn leather-bound volume the DEA agent had pulled from the shelf during his first search of the room.

"Tennyson's poems," she said, gesturing with the book—one of the original editions her father had collected—before she returned it to its place on the shelf.

"Better check it to be sure he didn't plant a listening device in it."

Not quite sure if he was teasing or not, Laini sighed. "I know I'm being unfair. He has a job to do. But he's so *blind*!"

The anger that had simmered in her since Weiss's first accusation of Glen boiled over without warning. Fury barely controlled sizzled through her like splashed water hissing on a hot stove. "He trusted Glen enough to leak information to him when Glen was writing those articles on drugs. How can he be so suspicious now? His informant was lying! Glen was the same man when he died that he'd always been!" Her heart felt as though a giant fist were squeezing it. "He didn't do anything wrong! I know he didn't!"

"So do I." D.J. spoke gruffly. "But Virge is one of the agency's best, Laini. And he was Glen's friend. He'll give Glen a fair shake, you can count on it."

"Well, he certainly doesn't act like he's doing it!"

Reaching for the phone at Glen's bedside, D.J. sat on the bed. Pulling her down beside her, he started dialing.

John Baz who had been Glen's editor for special assignments and, before D.J. had taken the desk job, his editor, too, seemed to take forever to answer his phone after the call had gone through the newspaper's switchboard.

Making good use of the time, D.J. fitted an arm around Laini's shoulders, trying in vain to convince himself it was so she could share the receiver with him. But the sensations her nearness evoked had nothing to do with either business or how he felt about what she was doing—was going to do—to Murphy. Rolling over his better judgment like a steamroller on hot asphalt, they left him ready to take her to bed and to hell with the consequences.

"John Baz here!" a crusty voice finally boomed in his ear.

"Hiya, John. D. J. Boone—"

"Funny you should call now. Hank's here with me. She picked up on something going on over at DEA I think you should hear."

"Something's going on here, too," D.J. said, as instinct he'd grown familiar with while chasing hard news sparked in his mind. "Virge Weiss, from the DEA's southeastern division, is here with blood in his eye."

Did Baz have any idea Weiss may have been Glen's fiercely protected "source inside the DEA" that Glen had sometimes quoted in his articles?

Laini's sharp intake of breath made him regret his choice of words, although he knew this wasn't something he could protect her from. Whatever Henrietta Langley had picked up on at the Drug Enforcement Administration Washington offices was probably going to hurt Laini; and there was nothing he could do about it, however much he wanted to shield her.

"I've got Glen's sister here with me," he continued, hoping that might cause Baz to be less explicit, and in the brief hesitation before Baz spoke, D.J. imagined him exchanging a knowing look with "Hank" Langley.

"Give her my best, D.J." Baz spoke slowly, as though selecting his words with utmost care. It made D.J. uneasy. "My deepest sympathy, and Hank's. Glen was a good man." Beside him, D.J. felt Laini getting a grip on herself, and he wanted to lay the phone down and hold her. Baz continued: "I'm putting you on the speaker phone now."

"You all right?" Silently D.J. mouthed the question to Laini, who nodded.

"Okay," he said aloud, speaking again to Baz. "We're sort of set up that way, too."

"I'll let Hank tell you." Baz seemed eager to get on with it.

"Right."

Henrietta Langley had been on the Washington scene longer than he and Baz put together, and she didn't fool around, with words or otherwise that he knew of. More important, her instincts were apt to be right on the button.

Speaking in her habitually borderline-raspy voice, she got right to it. "I've never seen DEA locked up so tight, D.J. I went over there to pick up a sidebar to the plane-crash story—follow-up stuff, some good human-interest quotes, reminiscences on the drug-related stories Glen had done when he was in Washington, contacts he'd had within the agency and, although I didn't really expect anyone to admit them, a plaudit or two."

She uttered an unladylike expletive. "The minute I mentioned Glen, they couldn't get me out the door fast enough. I could hear doors slamming all over the place, if you get what I'm saying."

"Gotcha," D.J. replied, and buried his face in Laini's short black curls, as much to draw strength from her as to give solace.

He'd seen it happen—not with the DEA, because that agency hadn't been his beat—but with the National Security Council and a couple of other offices. Nothing got a reporter's nose to the ground faster, but the bureaucrats never seemed to comprehend that fact.

"That's about all there is, right now." Baz broke into the silence. Then he added brusquely, "When will you be heading back to D.C.?"

Sensing an unspoken direct order, D.J. did some quick calculations. The memorial service was to be the morning of the day after tomorrow. If he left immediately afterward and drove straight through— "Put me down on your calendar and Hank's for nine on Friday morning. With luck you'll have something more to tell me by then."

"Nine on Friday it is," Baz agreed. And then, "Sorry about Glen, Miss Moran."

"Thank you." Laini's whisper told D.J. she didn't trust her voice.

He'd barely hung up the phone when Murphy popped into the room, a red-haired Jack-out-of-his-box with frightened blue eyes and Frog clutched to his middle like an anchor to hang on to in a storm raging around him.

"What's a war runt?"

"Murphy," Laini said gently without moving from D.J.'s embrace, "were you listening all that time? You must have been, if you heard about the search warrant."

Shifting from one sneakered foot to the other, Murphy nodded. "Was real careful. I didn't let the man see me."

"Murph," D.J. began, and stopped.

Holding out her arms, Laini said softly, "Come here, Murphy, honey. There's ... something we have to tell you."

Murphy held back, clutching Frog to the front of his T-shirt.

"'Bout that man?"

"Yes. And about Glen."

Appearing poised to bolt, Murphy burst out, "That man, he's bad!"

D.J. knew they'd lost him even before Laini asked "How do you know that?" Murphy's face closed up as though a window blind had been pulled down behind it. He was out of there like a shot.

When Laini made no move to leave the circle of his arm and follow, D.J. gave in to impulse and, bending his head, touched his lips to her throat—and left them there, savoring the quickened beat of her pulse that matched the drumming beat of his own heart.

"If there weren't more important things we both have to do," he murmured, his lips still brushing her warm flesh, wooing her sweetness into his soul, "I can think of a much better use for this bed than sitting on it while we make phone calls to editors."

Laini moved in his embrace, evoking in him such a rush of hunger for her that he wasn't sure he could deal with it. Lord, give me strength, he prayed, wanting nothing more than to lay her back and love her; let her love him with all the passion he felt was surging through her in response to his own desire.

"Who says 'more important?'" she whispered softly, moving again until her lips were breathtakingly near his own, immobilizing his good sense, to say nothing of his better judgment.

Lightly, briefly, she touched her lips to his.

"Just things that have to be done," she murmured.

An Indiana State Police car, a county sheriff's car and the black sedan Laini recognized as the rental car Weiss drove were parked in front of the house when she returned from the mortuary where she had made plans for the simple memorial Glen would have wanted.

Laini's heart sank. She had hoped to get into Glen's computer before the DEA agent returned with his search warrant. Hadn't he promised her until Friday, the day after the service?

Instantly she realized Weiss hadn't promised her anything. Sighing, she wondered how he had gotten the warrant so quickly.

D.J. was waiting when she parked behind his sports car in the driveway.

"Virge got his war runt," he said, mimicking Murphy. Holding the car door open, he gave her a hand out. Laini felt her spirits lift despite the ominous presence of the officers on the porch. "He's chomping at the bit."

"So let him chomp," she retorted. She was pleased that she sounded so calm and in control. "Did you find Murphy?"

Nodding, he answered, "Down at the brickworks. Guess it's a favorite place, with him. Seems he and Glen spent a lot of time down there. I, uh, think he feels closer to Glen when he's there."

Laini's throat threatened to close up.

Leaning closer as he shut the car door behind her, he asked, "Do you get the idea Murphy's scared of Virge?"

"Yes. And I'd like to know why."

"All right, all right, you two. Stop your lallygagging." Weiss sounded deceptively jovial. "This isn't the Spanish Inquisition, you know."

"You could have fooled me," Laini replied as she turned from D.J.'s near embrace. She glared at the DEA agent. "May I see the warrant, please?" she demanded as she squared off in front of him.

He handed it over. "Don't worry, it's legal."

"I don't doubt that it is."

Nodding to the other two officers, one of whom lived in Sycamore Point and looked as though he would rather be anywhere else at the moment, she then spoke to Miss Annie, who stood just inside the door with her thin arms folded across her chest. "It's all right, Miss Annie. Give them any assistance you can."

"What I'd like to give them," the housekeeper responded, sniffing audibly, "is a good dose of salts."

Weiss tsk-tsked. "That sounds like no more apple pie and coffee for yours truly."

Ignoring the obvious attempt at a pleasantry, Laini asked, "Where do we start?"

"You insist on doing this the hard way?"

"You bet I do," Laini said, steeling herself for the ordeal ahead. Virgil Weiss poking through Glen's possessions without her supervision was utterly unthinkable, no matter what his official status or how like a friend doing an unpleasant duty he wanted her to think he was.

Forgetting the anger that had sprouted between them over Murphy's future, she moved closer to D.J.

The DEA agent seemed to know what he was looking for, Laini admitted grudgingly. The search moved quickly from Glen's spacious living-work-bedroom to the library where—as Miss Annie confessed under questioning—Glen had worked often "at his daddy's old secretary."

And Virge had apparently briefed the state trooper and the deputy sheriff well; they concentrated on closets, bookshelves, the rest of the house, leaving the computer files and Glen's private papers for Weiss's perusal.

Weiss then searched the small newspaper building a quarter mile from the house, at the edge of town— so thoroughly that Laini expected him to start ripping off the weathered clapboards when he'd finished inside.

"If you'll tell me what you're looking for—" she tried again "—I might be able to help you."

She didn't really expect an answer, and she didn't get one.

D.J. squeezed the hand he'd held during much of the search, and she squeezed back. When he slipped his other arm around her waist and drew her against him, she felt a rush of warmth through her veins that was a long time cooling down.

The DEA agent took a final slow survey of the single partitionless room that looked much as it had when Laini and Glen's father had published his weekly newspaper there, then turned to Laini. He threw up both pudgy hands in an apparent admission of defeat.

"Clean as a whistle, so far." After studying her a moment, he said, "Relax, Laini."

"I'll relax when you admit this whole thing is a farce."

Weiss's sharp intake of breath hissed all the way to his lungs. "That's an unfair thing to say. No one wants Glen cleared more than I do."

"I doubt that."

Weiss seemed to hesitate, then shrugged. "You know how it is. We get a tip, we check it out. Glen would tell you that."

Although she cautioned herself it was a mistake, Laini let her body lean against D.J.'s. "I know that, Virgil," she admitted, trying to smile. It was hard when she knew the investigation was far from ended and the worst might lie ahead. "I suppose you have to do your job."

"Spoken like Glen Moran's sister," Virge replied, then hesitated a moment before he asked, "When did you say the memorial service is?"

She told him ten on Thursday morning at the Sycamore Point Funeral Home, and he nodded and left, pausing outside to speak briefly with the state trooper and deputy sheriff. The two officers had spent the last hour looking nervous and, Laini suspected, feeling useless. Weiss, she mused, had seemed afraid someone other than he might make a discovery.

After they left, D.J. drew her into his arms and kissed the corner of her mouth.

"I'm proud of you, Laini."

"You can show me better than that."

Her hands framed his face while she moved her mouth over his, tasting his lips with the tip of her tongue.

You're a brazen woman, Laini Moran, the little voice inside her accused.

But at least she was where she wanted to be—in D.J.'s arms, with his hands molding her body closer to his, his tongue wakening to stroke lovingly against hers. His lean, hard body registered promises she told herself were unreal and must remain so until this madness about Glen ended....

"What are you doing?" Murphy's reedy voice sounded very far away to Laini.

"Kissing Laini," D.J. replied, as he withdrew from Laini's mouth, leaving only a promise of the ecstasy she'd been on the verge of drowning in.

"Kissing D.J.," she said, struggling to get her breathing back to normal. Murphy did pick the darndest times to show up!

Although she had a feeling it may have been a good thing.

Looking as though he'd discovered his personal utopia, Murphy just stood there as though his sneakers were nailed to the worn threshold. Laini hated what she would have to tell him.

"Change your mind and come with me?"

The memorial service was over, and D.J. was preparing to leave for Washington.

"Sam can fly back, like he planned to do in the first place." Sam was one of the crowd of Glen's former colleagues who had come from all over the country and Europe to attend the service.

Laini shook her head. She wanted nothing more than to be with D.J., but she couldn't go. They had already discussed it. Too much remained unresolved. And for all that Weiss had turned Glen's things virtually inside out without finding whatever it was he sought, the answer to the charges against Glen might yet be in Sycamore Point . . . in this house.

If so, she intended to find it. And she hoped to make the discovery before Virge Weiss did.

"I'd like to, D.J. But I can't."

Glancing up from the suitcase he'd zipped shut, he smiled at her. His mesmerizing grin, half serious, half teasing, released butterflies in her stomach. "Can't you picture you, me, Murph doing the town?"

"That's the trouble," she confessed, willing the butterflies to settle down. "I can."

"Then give the kid a fling to remember before you stick him in a boarding school and forget about him."

"I will not forget him!" Laini flared in reply.

"Sure, you won't." D.J. checked the zipper on his luggage. "You'll pay his bills, send him presents and a check every month, see him a couple or three times a year, once when you take him on a high-falutin' vacation when the kid'd rather be in Sycamore Point with Frog and that speckled pup.

"C'mon, Laini—" he reached for her "—give the kid a break. Murph doesn't even have a grandmother to visit during Christmas and summer breaks and send him cookies made with love, like I did."

"What do you expect me to do?" Laini demanded, deftly eluding him. Folding her arms across her chest, she said, "Give up everything because—"

"Glen asked you to?" he finished softly when she broke off abruptly.

Gently his hands captured hers, opened her arms and lifted them up around his neck.

"Just don't do anything drastic until I get back."

Bending his head, he nibbled an earlobe, then moved to her throat, stringing little kisses like pearls, trailing a smoldering heat wherever his lips touched her.

"Promise?"

Shivering with delight she tried in vain to tell herself was unwelcome, she nodded. Willing strength that seemed about to forsake her, she placed her palms flat against his chest before the ache in her throbbing breasts revealed to him how very much she wanted him.

"D.J.," she began, but his mouth claimed hers, silencing her with a kiss that left her trembling. Hungrily her mouth followed his when he finally drew away from her.

"With our luck—" a smile began at the corners of his mouth and leaped magically to his eyes, bright with blue fire "—Murph'll come through that door any second."

Laini brushed a light kiss across his mouth and stepped away from him. "Call me as soon as you've talked with Baz and Hank."

Under the circumstances, it was the safest thing she could think to say—the *only* thing that wouldn't increase the turmoil that churned inside her.

Chapter Seven

If Glen was innocent?'' D.J. knew he sounded ready to jump down Baz's throat. ''Doesn't saying that make you feel like a Class A heel? You know damn well he was innocent!''

''I'll tell you how it makes me feel!'' Baz roared. ''Like a journalist!'' A cobra would look that way just before it struck, D.J. thought, meeting Baz's challenging gaze with a challenge in his own. ''Glen Moran's kind of journalist. *Yours*, too, I thought.''

''Okay, okay—'' D.J. raised both hands, palms facing outward, in a gesture of acquiescence ''—I'll do it.''

Lord help him if Laini found out, he thought. The Glen Moran story, with no punches pulled, could turn into a tiger by the tail before he was through with it. And if it did, Laini would either kill him or never let him touch her again. The latter, he decided, would be the worst fate of the two.

"If there's something going on over there in the DEA, we owe our readers the truth." The editor's glance flickered to Henrietta Langley, who had been in his office when D.J. arrived an hour earlier. "You ask me, it's damn strange they didn't find a trace of Glen where that plane crashed and burned. Makes me suspect a rotten egg in the custard."

D.J. stood abruptly. "Wouldn't be going for another Pulitzer, would you, Baz?"

Next time he saw the editor, he promised himself, it would be with a resignation from that desk job in hand. And as soon as he finished the special assignment, he'd quit the whole damn rat race.

Sycamore Point, here I come.

"Can we come on another picnic soon as D.J. gets back?" Murphy asked eagerly, helping himself to another hot dog.

Miss Annie had packed the basket of food at Laini's request when she gave up trying to get anything done with Murphy at her heels every minute as though he feared she would go away, too. He'd been like that since D.J.'s departure, drifting through the house like a small wraith.

"Sure," Laini said, hoping it would be soon. It was only noon Friday, less than twenty-four hours since D.J. had held her and kissed her as though he couldn't get enough of her, but already she missed him. She even missed arguing with him about Murphy.

"When is he coming back?"

"Soon, I hope," Laini answered.

Very, *very* soon, she hoped. She needed to get on with her life, and she had promised to wait until D.J.'s return before she spoke with Murphy—although she didn't for the life of her know why she had made the promise; Murphy was her responsibility, not D.J.'s.

"Are you going to marry him soon as he's home?"

"Murphy—" She tried to sound reproving but it was hard, the way her heartbeat had quickened. "We only met five days ago."

Murphy thought about that for all of twenty seconds. "Would you if he asked you?" His eyes, as blue as the October sky, were round and unblinking and infinitely pleading as they met hers.

"I'd have to think about it."

"Me and Frog want you to, so we can live with you, the way Glen said we could if anything happened to him. Glen said you'd raise me up, the way he was going to."

"I'll have to think about that, too, honey," Laini said, diving into the picnic basket and coming up with two red apples.

Silently handing one of them to him, she thought that she could just hear Glen reassuring the troubled little boy that he'd never be left alone again. It was the sort of thing an adult said when a child asked difficult questions—and she could imagine Murphy being full of difficult questions. And Glen had had so many good memories to share...so much to offer a waif like Murphy.

Feeling the sun warm on her face—feeling almost as if it were a reflection of Glen's smile—she leaned back against the crumbling brick wall.

What was she going to do?

Why not what Glen wanted? the tiny voice she heard sometimes from her innermost self inquired.

"Oh, yeah, sure," she muttered aloud, and then caught herself. Adopt Murphy and live in Sycamore Point?

You could do worse.

"Judge Elden was here the other day," she began, unsure where she was going with the conversation. "Do you remember him?"

"Yes'm." He stopped polishing his apple on the front of his T-shirt.

"He brought me a letter from Glen."

Murphy shot to his feet, running.

In total shock, Laini tossed her half-eaten apple to the blue jay that had been chattering from a nearby sycamore limb. She repacked the picnic basket, and then sat for a moment trying to figure out Murphy's reaction to what she'd said about a letter from Glen.

"Laini! *Laini!*"

The second "Laini!" was definitely nearer and more urgent than the first.

Calling out "Coming!" she quickened her naturally long stride, thinking that at least Murphy had recovered from whatever fright had sent him running away from her.

"Hur*ry!* D.J.'s calling from Washington!"

Her heart lurching into overdrive, Laini dropped the picnic basket and ran, narrowly missing crashing into a low-hanging branch and then Murphy, as he hurtled around a bend in the path.

"Get the basket, it's back there."

The words trailed over her shoulder. Unaccustomed to hundred-yard sprints, she arrived at the kitchen phone out of breath, her heart pounding so loudly D.J. should have heard it before her voice.

"D.J.!" she gasped. "Hi!"

"Hi, yourself." A chuckle whispered into her ear. "Where were you? I could have heard Murphy yelling all the way to D.C. without the phone."

Laini smiled. "We had a picnic down at the old brickworks. He—got back to the house first."

"Anything wrong?"

She should have known he'd pick up on the hesitation, she realized. "Not really. I made a boo-boo, I guess, I, uh, started to tell him about Glen's letter." Her sigh was audible. "He was off and running before I got three words out, and I don't know why."

"Take it easy with the kid, Laini. He's having enough of a rough time."

"Don't you think I know that?" Oh, heaven, why had she snapped at him?

"I know you do." A pause. "I'm going to need most of next week here, Laini. Fridays and weekends are lousy times to get hold of anybody in this town." Another hesitation. "You all right?"

Out of the corner of her eye she saw Murphy lug the picnic basket into the kitchen and motioned him to come to her.

To D.J. she said, "Murphy's here now." Leaning over, she held the phone so Murphy could hear, too.

"Hi again, Murph."

"When are you coming home?" Murphy sounded so wistful Laini wanted to hug him.

"In a few days. You take good care of Laini for me, you hear?"

"I asked her if she was gonna marry you if you asked her to."

"What did she say?" Laini went warm all over at the amusement in D.J.'s voice.

"She'd have to think about it."

"I'll think about it, too, Murph."

"All right, you two," Laini protested lightly, and D.J. laughed—a deep-throated sound that teased her senses even long-distance.

They talked for several minutes, with Laini wondering what he was leaving out. Something, that was for sure, she thought, but she didn't inquire until Murphy gave her a shy grin and vanished.

"Murphy's gone," she told D.J. "What have you really found out that you're not telling me?" she asked.

"Two things. As Virge said, first the bad news." At his ragged breath, a Klaxon sounded in Laini's mind. "There's a chance Glen was in D.C. late in July."

"Weren't you there then?"

"Yes. I'd just gotten back to Washington after being in Sycamore Point.

"There must be some mistake," she protested hoarsely. Glen in Washington and D.J., his best friend, hadn't known? She couldn't believe that.

"I hope you're right." D.J.'s tone was brusque. "But the way Hank Langley says the receptionist she was talking to over at the DEA yesterday clammed up when her boss came into the office, I'd say not.

"The question is: what was so big a secret about him being there that it's got the whole agency locked up tighter than a drum? You'd think they were sitting on one of their own blisters and didn't want the press to find out."

Laini heard the faint sound of breathing that wasn't her own or D.J.'s. "Murphy?"

"M-me and Frog—we—we wanted to say bye to D.J."

"Murph—"

"Don't yell at him, D.J.," Laini interrupted. Knowing Murphy's penchant for eavesdropping, they both should have expected something of the sort.

"Who's going to yell? Murph, why don't you and Laini hop on a plane and come to D.C.? We'll go to the zoo and the space museum—"

Somewhere in the house, Murphy dropped the extension in its cradle.

"What the hell'd I say wrong?" D.J. demanded.

Laini inhaled deeply. "I don't know, but I think I should go find him. He's a mixed-up little boy. What's the other thing?" she asked.

"I'm giving serious thought to chucking my job. Going free-lance. Tell you about it when I see you," he said hastily. "Take care, Laini."

"You too," she echoed, and hung up, wondering how such an unromantic conversation could excite her so.

Laini spent the remainder of the day and most of the weekend trying unsuccessfully to coax Murphy out of his shell. The rest of the time she went through Glen's possessions and arranged her own affairs so she could stay in Sycamore Point for longer than the week or ten days she had planned on being there.

Her news director was aghast. "You know what you're doing, don't you, Laini? You're putting your career at risk! The word's come down. The brass is ready to move you to New York. I'd hate to see anything happen now, for your sake."

"I'm not staying forever, Les. There's...something I have to take care of."

"Yeah, I know. Charley Lowrie faxed a memo somebody at the DEA in Atlanta slipped him."

Her heart constricting, Laini said, "Then you know what it is I have to do. Glen was innocent. I have to prove it."

The news director grunted. "Tell you what, kid. You're on assignment as of now. I'll get on the horn to New York and tell them both you and the story are worth waiting for."

"Thanks, Les."

"Ask for help from any of our affiliates whenever you need to. You'll get it."

Laini thanked him again and hung up, wishing she dared let herself cry. A memo leaked to a newsman from inside the DEA in Atlanta—she'd bet that had really burned Weiss. The investigation he was trying to keep under wraps being faxed to an L.A. television station.

And where else?

Her heart sank. Any hour now, the story would break across the country.

"Were you talking to D.J.?" Murphy spoke from so close beside her that she jumped.

Shaking her head, she explained, "My boss at the TV station in Los Angeles. I just fixed it so I can stay longer."

"Forever?" His eyes pleaded with her.

"Well—" Oh, dear heaven. Why did he have to be so appealing? "No. Not forever, darling." Why had she promised D.J. to wait before talking with Murphy? Now would be the perfect time.

"Till D.J. gets home?"

"Yes."

Holding Frog, the boy darted away from her. Moments later, the back door slammed, and almost at once, Fruitful's pups set up their customary hue and cry at the sight of Murphy.

Laini found the telephone book and looked up the Indiana State Police trooper's home phone.

"This is Laini Moran. I'm sorry to bother you on a Sunday afternoon," she began when he answered.

"That all right, Miss Moran. What can I do for you?"

Laini told him, and felt her spirits lift when he answered, "As far as I know, drug use in Sycamore Point is pretty penny-ante—a little marijuana, mostly kids experimenting. Although a year or so ago, we busted a guy for growing marijuana up in the bottoms."

"What about rumors of the truck stop being used as or being set up to become a major cocaine distribution point?"

"Hadn't heard that till Weiss showed up." She sensed a shrug in his voice.

"Can you give me a name in the local drug taskforce?"

"Glen asked me that."

Excitement leaped through her. "When?"

The officer hesitated. "It's like I told Weiss, I don't remember exactly. Sometime last summer. July—late July, maybe early August. Glen and I talked a lot about cocaine and crack and PCP. He said he was glad to be out of Washington where buying the stuff was as easy as buying soda pop." A pause. "You're not getting any ideas about getting into Weiss's investigation, are you?"

"Not the way you think. I'm going to prove Glen was clean and rub the DEA's nose in it. Virgil Weiss's nose to be specific, even if he is just doing his job."

The ISP trooper started laughing. "Go for it, Miss Moran." He stopped laughing. "Strictly off the record, you need any help, give me a call."

Laini promised to do just that, thanked him and hung up.

Now, she thought, her spirits lifting, she would call D.J.

With Murphy in school until three in the afternoon, Laini threw herself into searching the house from fruit cellar and potato bin to attic. She met again with Judge Elden, hung out at the truck-stop restaurant hoping through casual conversation to learn something—about Murphy's appearance out of the blue, about drug dealing, about Glen.

On Wednesday—armed with a description of Glen's car, its distinctive Back Home Again In Indiana bumper sticker and a set of duplicate keys that Miss Annie produced from a drawer in the kitchen—she drove to the Evansville airport where she returned the rental car and picked up Glen's Buick. He'd left the car there before taking off for Atlanta, in the short-term parking area—an indication to her that he had expected to return soon.

"You're a little late," the attendant remarked pleasantly when Laini handed him the ticket she'd found clipped to the sun visor.

"Someone was supposed to pick it up." Her heart wrenched at the truth of the words. "I . . . don't suppose anyone did try and had forgotten his key, or something?" She'd stumbled onto helpful information with such seemingly innocuous questions before.

Answering her query, the attendant shook his head as he told her the amount of the overdue tab.

Laini paid him, said thanks, and drove off wondering how Weiss, who had been so thorough everywhere else, had missed Glen's car. She'd half expected to find the car impounded until the investigation was over.

Mulling over that, and making lists in her head as she always did when she was working on a story, Laini traveled back to Sycamore Point hoping to make it home ahead of Murphy. Since the memorial service, Miss Annie had resumed her two-days-a-week housekeeper schedule.

A main artery between Miami, Atlanta and Chicago, U.S. 41's four busy lanes linked Sycamore Point with the world. Murphy *might* be from Florida, Judge Elden had told her when he'd reported on his efforts to learn Murphy's background.

But she had trouble picturing an eight-year-old boy hitching rides over such a long distance without someone notifying the authorities.

How she wanted to ask him how he had managed.

But she would wait, as Miss Annie said the child psychologist Glen had consulted had suggested, until Murphy brought up the subject himself.

A station wagon loaded for bear stood in front of the house when she drove up. Her heart gave a wild lurch when she saw D.J. back away from it, his arms loaded with books.

"All my worldly goods," he said, gesturing at the wagon when he'd dropped the books onto the driver's seat and was striding toward her.

Surprising her, he swept her into his arms the instant she was out of the car. "I'll be happy to endow you with them any time you say the word."

Unable to stop herself, Laini melted against him. "Have you been talking to Murphy again?"

"Where is he."

"School."

As though he'd been waiting for the word, D.J.'s mouth descended on hers. Laini hadn't realized how much she had missed him, how much she'd wanted him to do exactly what he was doing—parting her lips with his tongue and searching out her hunger for him, claiming her in every way but the sweet ultimate.

Her arms went around his neck, her fingers clutched at the mahogany forest at his nape. Her body clung to his, inviting his hands to fit her closer.

"Sorry, Laini." His voice sounded trapped deep in his throat. Gently his lips brushed hers. "Didn't intend to lose it."

"You're not the only one who lost it," she said as she rose on her toes and nibbled at his bottom lip. "And I'm not sorry," she added.

His palm slid down from the small of her back and pressed her hips against him. Sensations of warmth and desire crashed through her, shattering remnants of her resolve.

"D.J.!"

At Murphy's glad cry, Laini gasped. D.J.'s hand dropped from her breast as though her flesh had burned him. Smoothing her sweater with shaking hands, she struggled to breathe evenly.

"Hi, Murph."

With the greeting, D.J. swung the boy into the air as though he were four years old instead of eight and gave him a bear hug on the way down. "Aren't you supposed to be in school?"

Eloquent eyes pleaded for understanding as they clung to Laini's. "My stomach hurts."

"Did your teacher call Miss Annie to come for you? Is she here with you now?" Laini asked as she knelt in front of him, feeling suddenly helpless. Was it something he'd eaten? "Have you taken Pepto?"

"You're not mad at me?"

Laini hugged him. "Of course we're not mad at you, darling." Murphy's response to her barrage of questions was a dead giveaway. He had no more stomachache than she did. "Did you tell your teacher you were leaving school?"

Murphy looked at his sneakers.

"Murphy," she began reprovingly, "you shouldn't have left without telling her. You shouldn't be alone in the house, either."

"Nothing happened."

"But—" She stopped short of saying that something could have. She'd seen the results of too many children having been left alone. And Sycamore Point mightn't be the same wonderfully safe place for a child to grow up that it had been during her childhood.

"Couple of packages in there for you, Murph." D.J. nodded toward the station wagon, which appeared loaded to its dome light. "One's for you, the other's got Frog's name on it. Dig 'em out," he suggested, winking at the boy, "while I ask Laini something big."

"Are you going to ask her to marry you?"

"I don't think she's ready for that, Murph," D.J. said before Laini could speak.

With a look of disappointment on his freckled face, Murphy dived into the wagon, leaving Laini feeling vaguely disappointed herself, although she knew what her answer would have been.

What would it be, she wondered, if he asked her to live with him? She wasn't ready for that, either. Too much of her dream still waited for her.

Taking her arm, D.J. walked her a few feet away from the wagon before he spoke.

"Are you?"

"Is that your big question?"

The lopsided grin beguiled her senses. "No. Just thought I'd ask it since it seems to be Murphy's favorite question."

Laini smiled and waited for the big question she dreaded having to answer. *I don't want to lose you, D.J. But I'm not ready to live with you, either.*

When a faintly abrasive finger touched her cheek, she braced herself. *Oh, D.J., please understand when I say no.*

The finger traced a caressing path down her cheek to her mouth, his warm gaze following it. Laini's nerves tingled. He was going to kiss her again, and she wasn't ready for that, either.

"Will you lease or sell this place to a guy who's got one assignment, a book in his head and small town in his blood?"

"The way I see it," D.J. said hours later, after they had unloaded the station wagon, talked with Judge Elden whom Laini had invited to dinner, and then, when the judge had left and Murphy was in bed, settled down in front of a fire in the library to talk it all over again. "You're not ready to make a commitment to either Murphy or me. This way, I can be here for Murph."

She'd gotten over her initial surprise. "I may not want to sell the house. Don't forget, there's an awful lot of me in this house, in this town."

D.J. grinned at her. "I'm counting on that."

"Don't start," Laini warned, making a face at him.

Leaning back in the leather chair that had been old when her father had inherited it from his father, she sighed. "If growing up in Sycamore Point weren't what Glen wanted for Murphy, I'm not sure I'd think of leaving him, even with you."

"You know what Glen really wanted."

"I can't stay here!" The words burst past her lips. "Glen had no right to ask."

"Maybe not." D.J., who had been standing with his back to the fire, reached for her hands and drew her to her feet, into his arms. "But you're his sister, his only family. He loved you, and he loved Murphy."

His gaze locked with hers. "You can't blame him for wanting the best possible for both of you."

The tears she'd managed to control until now suddenly felt very close to spilling over. To stop the flow, she buried her face against his shoulder. "Oh, D.J.," she whispered, "how can life get so complicated?"

"You gotta come quick!"

Clutching Frog to his pajama top, Murphy catapulted into the library.

"Glen's come back! Me and Frog, we just heard him in his room!"

Chapter Eight

Oh, honey,'' Laini exclaimed softly, opening her arms to Murphy as she knelt in front of him,'' it was just a dream!''

Murphy squirmed away from her. "Wasn't a dream!'' he protested. Eyes wide and fearful, he appeared ready to bolt. "Glen's back—he's in his room! Me and Frog, we heard him!''

Laini's glance leaped to D.J. Oh, God. What would a burglar hope to find in Glen's room *now*?

"Don't suppose there's a baseball bat handy?'' D.J. sounded incredibly calm.

She shook her head. If there was, she didn't know where it was.

"You and Murphy stay here,'' D.J. told them.

Before heading for the door, he reached for the fireplace poker. "Might be a good idea to call Dan Boles.'' The ISP officer lived a short distance away.

Huddling closer to her, Murphy whispered, ''D.J.'s not going to hurt Glen, is he?''

Burying her face in the child's thatch of tousled red hair, Laini whispered, ''Murphy, honey, nothing can hurt Glen now. Not if we go on believing in him.''

But could she do that? If Glen hadn't been involved in something terrible, why was someone so interested in his room after Weiss—and she—had turned it inside out?

You'd almost think, she speculated, that whatever Glen had been involved in—however he was involved in it—Weiss was in it, too, and was trying to find something before someone else did.

Glen's room might not have appeared such a shambles if she hadn't spent much of the previous day going through everything in it and leaving it exactly as she knew it had been before Weiss's search: as neat as a pin.

Now, a desk drawer stood open an inch and papers on top of the desk were in disarray. Books were every which way on the shelves. Closets appeared to have been hit by a windstorm only slightly less violent than a tornado.

The bed looked as though it had been made in a hurry, and if she'd been taught anything, it had been to turn corners neatly and leave the spread and the pillow shams smooth and inviting to the eye.

An open window testified to a hasty exit.

''Haven't touched anything, have you?'' the ISP officer asked after he had looked around the room.

"No," she and D.J. answered in unison.

When Murphy remained silent, clinging to her hand as though he still feared he'd heard Glen back from the dead, Laini prompted, "Murphy, darling, did you touch anything?"

Murphy shook his head. "I didn't go in there."

The officer dropped to one knee, putting his face on a level with Murphy's.

"Don't be afraid, Murphy. You did good, you used your head in a dangerous situation." A pause. "Now, I want you to think about what you heard so you can tell me in a little while. Will you do that for me?"

Murphy nodded.

Giving him an approving pat on the shoulder, the trooper said as he stood up, "I need to radio for a print team and backup." He glanced at D.J. "Want to come out to the car with me, Mr. Boone?"

What did he want to say to D.J. that he thought he couldn't tell her—or say in front of Murphy? "Do you think the intruder is still around?"

"Doubtful. But on the chance he may be, Mr. Boone will be where he can observe that window while I'm on the car radio."

Still clutching the poker as though he intended to use it on the first shadow that moved, D.J. touched her cheek tenderly with the back of his other hand, then left with the officer.

She and Murphy followed them into the hall.

The phone rang as they neared the library. Expecting Harley Bensinger or another neighbor who had seen the police car out front, she answered on the third ring.

"Laini—" Virgil Weiss's wheezy voice rumbled in her ear "—I'm in a phone booth on I-75 outside Alachua. Been trying to reach Deej in D.C. Is he back there, by any chance?"

The words poured out, half drowned in the whine of tires on the highway and the blasting horn of a passing diesel truck.

"Yes. But I can't get him now, Virgil. The police are here. Do you want—"

"What the hell the police there for?" Weiss's voice thundered in her ear.

Thinking that he needn't bellow, she told him what had happened, then asked again if he wanted D.J. to call him back.

"Naaa. I'm on a stakeout."

"Virgil—" Laini hesitated, wondering if she should voice her new suspicion.

"Gotta go, Laini! My guy's comin' outa the motel!"

The connection was broken.

Hanging up, Laini turned to Murphy. A breath caught in her throat.

Every freckle on the boy's face appeared painted on, he was so pale. She knelt in front of him. "Don't be frightened," she said gently. "Whoever was in Glen's room is probably long gone by now."

When he seemed not to have heard her, she suggested, "Let's go make some hot chocolate." With an inaudible sigh, she decided it was going to be a long night.

"What did he want?" Murphy asked.

"To talk to D.J. They've known each other a long time, Murphy." She'd thought he was worrying about the prowler. "They're both working to prove Glen's innocence." *I hope.* "Virge may have found out something he wants to tell D.J."

Wishing she believed that, she wondered if Weiss knew about the DEA in Washington being "locked up tighter than a drum," and what it would mean if he did—that Glen had been involved in some sort of undercover work again. Heaven knew, he'd done it often enough before, she thought.

"He could have told you, couldn't he?"

"I don't know why he didn't tell me, honey," she admitted. "Sometimes people don't say things they should."

With a strangled sob, Murphy buried his face against her.

"Oh, darling, I know," she whispered, instinctively holding him closer. "It *hurts!*"

Dawn was a misted gray light outside the window when Laini woke the next morning, with Murphy curled like a contented puppy beside her. A smile curved her lips, warming her to the depths of her soul. She'd sure become a parent in a hurry!

Then she remembered last night, and the happiness that swelled through her turned as cold as the windowpanes looked with rain pelting against them.

October in southern Indiana could be fickle, rushing toward winter while still holding on to the last remnants of summer. This morning, it appeared, winter was near.

The police hadn't found a trace of the intruder, and she, Laini thought, was willing to bet there wouldn't be a fingerprint that wasn't hers, D.J.'s, Murphy's, Miss Annie's, or, from that earlier search, Weiss's.

But someone definitely had been in Glen's room.

She hoped she'd finally convinced Murphy it hadn't been Glen's spirit rattling around looking for something he'd left behind. Where did eight-year-old boys pick up such ideas, anyway?

"If you're not awake, you've got the most expressive face of any woman I've ever watched sleep."

Laini's eyes popped open. How could she have forgotten that Murphy had refused to go to bed unless she and D.J. were in his bed with him? She'd planned to go to her own room as soon as the child was asleep.

"Shh," she cautioned in a whisper. "You'll wake up Murphy."

"Not unless you do."

The breath caught in her throat when he raised himself on an elbow, sending the blanket tumbling, baring a mat of curling chest hair. She met him halfway, her lips hungry for his.

Slow, sensuous kiss was traded for slow, sensuous kiss. The energy building within her neared an emotion that threatened to consume every shred of her self-control.

And she mustn't permit it. She could fall in love with D.J.—she already had, she feared. But now was not the time to admit it, and not the time to let it happen. Maybe in a year or two, she thought; when she'd reached her goal, had had a year or two on the anchor desk.

"D.J.," she whispered when, finally, his mouth drew away from hers. His eyes continued their tender assault, scattering sparks that burst like an exploding wildfire through her. "We have to talk."

"It's likely that statement is the world's most famous morning-after line," he quipped teasingly.

"About what happened last night."

D.J. grinned broadly. "You went to sleep before Murph did. Nothing happened last night."

"You know what I mean."

Taking care not to wake Murphy, she slipped out of bed and tucked the blanket around him, trying in vain to keep her gaze off D.J.'s bare chest.

If anything had happened last night, she might have slept afterward with her cheek against his chest, she mused in spite of herself—and felt cheated. It would have been a memory to treasure during the long, empty nights ahead.

Moving with animal grace that threatened to further devastate her already shaken control, D.J. swung long, trouser-clad legs from under the blanket and stood up. He reached for the shirt he'd removed sometime during the night.

"I wish I didn't know what you meant, but I do," he said, shrugging into the shirt. His hands hesitated on the buttons. "Couldn't interest you in doing this for me, could I?" His husky tone and bold, teasing glance continued the seduction.

Feeling giddy, with her senses trapped in enchantment, she broke eye contact with an effort. Murphy was stirring.

Before he came fully awake, she murmured hastily, "I'll make coffee," and fled.

A precocious eight-year-old's insight into her emotions she couldn't deal with, now. She wasn't sure she could deal with her own.

Never had she wanted a man in the many ways she wanted D.J.—with "forever" heading the list. *Never* had she met one she expected to have more trouble saying no to.

After putting the coffee on, Laini went to her room where she showered, blow-dried her short black hair and dressed in fresh jeans and a warm cashmere sweater. The chill accompanying the rain that had begun after midnight seemed to have crept into her bones—when she'd thought nothing could ever make her feel so cold or so afraid again.

Shuddering at the thought of anyone boldly entering Glen's room while Murphy slept in the next room and she and D.J. were in the library, she paused outside the room. Who had been in there last night? *Why?*

The police had sealed the room after their unsuccessful search of it and the ground outside the open window. What had Glen hidden so well that neither

Weiss—if Weiss hadn't merely been putting on a good show—nor she or the police had found it?

What was so important that someone else had come after it?

When she returned to the kitchen, D.J. was there, a mug of coffee at his elbow, the morning newspaper up in front of his face.

"Is it appropriate to say good-morning after we've slept together?" His soft west Texas drawl teased her from behind the paper.

"We did *not* sleep together."

Folding the newspaper, D.J. laid it beside his place.

"To tell you the truth, I didn't do much sleeping." His big hand smothered a yawn. "What do you make out of last night?"

Crossing the kitchen, she poured herself a mug of coffee, then spent more time than was necessary stirring nondairy creamer into it.

Back at the table, she sat down across from him.

"You knew Glen better than I did, these last few years." An audible sigh crept past her lips. "Do you know how much it hurts to admit that?"

With both hands, she lifted the mug to her lips. "I didn't even know my own brother." After a tentative sip, she set the mug down. "We used to be so close. I feel as if I've failed him, let him down, somehow."

D.J. shook his head. "Glen was an adult. He'd been making his own decisions for a long time. Whatever he was thinking when he bought that plane and took off for Atlanta, it was his decision to do it. What I'd like to know is, why the lock-down at DEA?"

"Well, I aim to find out," Laini declared, taking another swallow of coffee that tasted like gall despite the creamer she'd stirred into it.

"That won't be easy."

"So what? Glen never backed off from a good story in his life, and I'd like to think I won't. I intend to find out what he was doing in that plane. Was he working on a story? Maybe he was undercover, although you can't expect Weiss or anyone else to admit it...." She paused for a moment. "If he was, as Virge says, into drug trafficking, then I will find out the truth."

Drawing a deep breath, she let it put out the fire in her before she spoke again.

"Does that make any sense at all?"

Both of D.J.'s hands came across the table to cradle hers, which clasped the coffee mug as though her life depended on having something solid to hang on to.

"Like you said, honey—" his voice was rough with his own emotion, but so caring it was like a caress "—we have to talk."

"Do I have to go to school today?"

Rubbing sleep from his eyes, Murphy stood in the doorway, clutching Frog, as usual, in one hand against his middle. The frog appeared faintly damp from having spent the night in the aquarium.

Smiling, Laini opened her arms to him and said, "Come give me a hug." She hadn't even thought about school.

He fairly leaped toward her, hugging her with one arm while the other hand still held Frog. Somehow Frog wound up brushing against her breast.

"Never thought I'd envy a bullfrog," D.J. growled, sparks dancing in his eyes as his gaze locked with hers. Laini was certain she turned flamingo pink all over. "Hey, Murph," D.J. asked him, chuckling, "don't I get a hug?"

If this was a sample of what her life could be with the two of them, Laini reflected, she'd take all of it she could get and to heck with the anchor job.

But reality pounced.

You just now vowed to find out the truth about Glen, whatever it might be, her other, inner self reminded her. *You can't walk away into the sunset in the next breath, with Murphy hanging happily on to one hand and D.J. whispering sweet love in your ear.*

She couldn't do it even if she did owe a debt to Glen.

"Tell you what, Murphy—" Rallying her common sense, she wondered what a child psychologist would say about striking a deal with an eight-year-old child. "We'll forget school today if you'll help us look for something Glen may have hidden so it would be safe."

"Glen didn't hide stuff."

"Maybe not from you, Murph," D.J. said easily, shifting the boy to his other knee. "He might have, from someone he didn't like or trust. Do you know anybody like that?"

Laini held her breath. Had there been an almost imperceptible change in Murphy's manner?

"Glen didn't do bad things neither. Don't care what that man says."

"Oh, honey, of course he didn't," Laini exclaimed. Murphy, his small chin jutting, pressed his lips together tightly. He was the picture of defiance. "We know that. But we still have to prove it to people who don't understand why he bought that airplane he didn't need."

Wondering if the child understood what she was saying, she hesitated. How could she expect him to grasp what had gone on with Glen when neither D.J., Miss Annie or Judge Elden, who'd known him so well and for so long, couldn't figure it out?

"What do you want me to do?"

Laini's heart beat faster. Well, what did she want?

Dare she hope he could answer her questions about the weeks immediately before Glen's death? The answers she needed would be next to impossible for him to provide.

How could he know where Glen had gotten the money to buy an airplane capable of flying nonstop from deep in the Caribbean to southern Indiana? Or if Glen had been working on a story about drugs in Sycamore Point? Or if the plane and the trip to Atlanta were links to the South American drug rings, as Weiss believed? They weren't subjects Glen would have discussed with an eight-year-old child.

"I don't know," she confessed. "Tell us about Glen, I guess. Things you saw him working on, things he may have asked you to help him with. Or what the two of you talked about when you walked in the woods or down along the river." Glen would have done that with him, she was certain. "Places he took you. People who came to see him."

Guilt stabbed through her. She might be asking the child to betray her own brother—the man who had been kind to him, offered him a home—and she hated herself for doing it.

In the kennel out back, Fruitful bayed. Immediately the pups took up the cry.

"Damn dogs," D.J. grumbled as he lifted Murphy off his knees. "Why couldn't they have made a ruckus like that last night when there was something to bark at?" Opening the door, he straightened in obvious surprise that sent a start leaping through Laini.

"Virge. I thought Laini said you called from Florida."

"I did."

Shaking rain off his hat, he came into the kitchen without waiting for an invitation, talking as he came. "I got our man right after that, and hopped a plane soon as the paperwork was done." Scarcely pausing for breath, he demanded, "What were the police doing here? Did they catch anybody?"

Wishing she could disappear as quickly as Murphy, who seemed to have melted into the woodwork the moment D.J. said Virge's name, she told him what had happened the previous night.

Weiss muttered an oath. "I guess that's what I get for thinking I'd do better looking down in Florida. But then again, I may have, depending on what we shake out of that druggie in Alachua. We got his name from the same tipster who turned Glen in."

With a wheezy cough, he continued: "That doesn't change things here. Whatever's in this house, I aim to be the laddie that finds it."

Anger she'd managed to control until now flared through Laini. "When are you going to tell us precisely what it is you're looking for, Virgil? And who your informant is?"

"You know that as much as I want to, I can't release that information."

Shrugging out of his trench coat, Weiss tossed the garment across a chair, then sat down on another one. Laini wondered why she believed him. He hadn't given her much reason to trust him.

"In case you're wondering why I came 'round to the back door," he went on, looking from her to D.J. and again at Laini, "I took a look around outside. Seems as though the rain has done a pretty good job of messing up any tracks that might have been left."

"You didn't help any by tromping around."

"Now, Laini," he chided mildly, "you don't have to worry about me fouling up the scene of a crime." His grin was wide. "How about a cup of java to take the chill off?"

It'd take more than that for her, Laini thought as she poured the coffee. Even when he was apparently working hard at being friendly, she couldn't help the feeling that Virgil Weiss was holding something back—something about Glen that she needed to know.

Even with the police continuing their investigation of the break-in, Laini had anticipated pleasant snatches of time alone with D.J. Rainy days and crackling fires evoked visions of romance in spite of her stern self-reminders that they'd best stick to talk about his decision to stay in Sycamore Point.

Weiss's arrival changed everything. The man seemed to be everywhere at once. If he wasn't asking questions, he was barking orders at the state police and sheriff's officers as though Sycamore Point were his jurisdiction. Or he was pawing through Glen's possessions and scanning everything in his computer as though he hadn't done all that already.

He might, she thought more than once, have been playing a role. But in the name of heaven, *why*? If Glen had been undercover, part of a DEA sting operation, why couldn't *she* have been told? *Be told now?*

Finally it was over.

"I don't blame Murphy for staying in his room," Laini remarked as she and D.J. stood at one of the library windows watching the officers pause for one last, brief huddle before they climbed into their cars. "Or you for pulling up the drawbridges."

"Is that what I've done?"

"It's what I felt you were doing."

Slipping a hand into one of his, she felt some of the tension that had nagged at her all day drain away and a new, explosive energy build to take its place.

"Are you all right?" she asked softly. He had seemed so withdrawn all day.

Nodding, he said, "I'll be better when we figure out last night."

Brushing a kiss across her temple, D.J. pulled her against him. His hands moved under her sweater and his fingertips began a sensuous exploration of her rib cage, caressing her satiny skin, generating exciting sensations. Encountering the silk and lace of her bra, they halted.

"I've wanted you all day," he whispered hoarsely. "Wanted to touch you." With poignant tenderness, his hands moved to cover her breasts, stroking through the wispy fabric. "Wondering how it would feel to kiss you there. And there."

"Is he gone?"

Laini's breath stopped. Her heart skipped a beat. Neither might have resumed if D.J., sounding as choked as she felt, hadn't spoken when he did.

"Yes, Murphy. He's gone."

"When's he coming back?"

Rearranging her sweater as unobtrusively as possible, Laini got breathing space between herself and D.J. before she turned to meet Murphy's questioning gaze.

If her face wasn't as pink as a flamingo it was a miracle.

"I don't know, Murph," D.J. answered, as his index finger, which had wrecked such sensual havoc at her breast, touched her throat and began a slow seduction of the throbbing pulse below her ear.

Laini wondered if he knew how badly she wanted to feel his lips there, instead; how badly she wanted him to continue the interrupted attention to her breasts, although she was far from certain how much longer she could have maintained control if he had.

Capturing his adoring hand, she put a stop to the fire he was lighting in her.

Moistening her parched lips, she said huskily, "He's going to help the police find the person who was in Glen's room, honey. And maybe find what he was after."

"Me and Frog, we know."

"What!" D.J. burst out, drowning Laini's sharp intake of breath.

With a vigorous nod, Murphy shifted from one foot to the other. Frog, nestled in both his hands against the fleece-lined sweatshirt that, with the colder weather, had replaced a T-shirt as his favorite attire, looked definitely more comfortable than his master.

"It's all right, Murphy," Laini said softly, dropping to her knees in front of him. "You can tell us. What is it?"

"Don't know exactly what."

Her heart sank. Not a speck of dust in Glen's room had escaped scrutiny. Weiss had searched the room twice; she had gone through everything. What could someone have hoped to find?

"Where?" she asked. "Do you know that?"

"In his computer."

And Weiss had had first crack at that. Laini smothered a few choice words. Aloud she said, "Did he show you what he was working on? Or tell you anything about it?" She smiled. "Like maybe a story about how you and Frog came to Sycamore Point and met each other here?" She could imagine Glen, always a good storyteller, doing that.

"Glen didn't know about me—"

In a sudden widening of his blue eyes, she saw his quick mind hit the brakes. "Can me and Frog go now?"

He darted away almost before she said "Sure."

She rose, into D.J.'s waiting arms.

"Where were we?" he asked hoarsely as his mouth descended towards hers.

"What didn't Glen know about how Murphy came to Sycamore Point? I thought he found him scrounging in the dumpster at the truck stop. What's the big secret about how he got there?"

D.J. kissed her lightly, then asked, "What's with Murph and Virge?" He pulled away from her and his long fingers combed through his mahogany hair. "My grandmother used to say kids had instincts about people the rest of us have lost in the growing up, but it sure isn't working that way with Murph."

He continued after a pause. "You should see Virge with those kids of his—his and hers, guess I should say. Glen used to say Virge would sell his soul if he thought the money he'd get for it would help him provide for them better than he could do on a DEA agent's salary."

"Maybe he did."

Drawing her back into his arms, he kissed her again—not so lightly.

"Take my word for it, love," he said when he lifted his mouth from hers, "Virge is honest as the day is long, and he's a teddy bear with his family."

She drew a Cupid's bow on his mouth with the tip of a finger and, rising on tiptoe, traced the path of the bow with the tip of her tongue. "If you say so."

But what if Murphy was right and Virge was "bad"? What if Glen had known, and Virge wanted the evidence of his guilt before someone else found it?

Chapter Nine

Laini! D.J.!"

At the sound of Murphy's voice, she and D.J. sprang apart as though they were teenagers caught making out at the senior prom.

"Come see!"

"Now what?" D.J. muttered against her lips, drowning out the rest of Murphy's summons.

Covering her ears with both his hands, he shouted, "Coming, Murph!" And he kissed her again, lightly and quickly, but promisingly. Definitely that. "Let's go find out what he wants."

Tasting his kiss with the tip of her tongue, she tried not to think that Murphy's timing was for the birds.

He'd sounded...strange. A vague uneasiness stirred in the pit of her stomach.

"Hur-ry!" The plea was oddly muffled.

They found him on his back with only his sneakers showing from under the edge of the sturdy base Harley Bensinger had built for Glen's aquarium when Glen had been about Murphy's age.

Her heart pounding, Laini dropped to her stomach and peered under the table. "What have you found, honey?" she asked the gamin face that peered back at her from the gloom.

"You'll have to scrootch under on your back to see."

Not sure there was room enough, Laini rolled over onto her back. Standing over her, D.J. looked ten feet tall, a god come down from Olympus and liking what he saw. Excitement that had nothing to do with Murphy's find skirled through her.

Hastily she got her head and shoulders beneath the table. It was like being at the bottom of a well and it took her eyes a couple of seconds to adjust to the difference in light. Then she inhaled sharply. Taped to the underside of the tabletop was a jacketed computer disk in a clear plastic envelope.

"Want me to turn Frog loose and help to get it?" Murphy held the frog aloft in both hands, obviously reluctant to release it unless she asked him to. "I had to crawl under to catch him."

Laini wriggled farther under the aquarium base. It was a close fit.

"I think I can reach it now." She slid a finger under the plastic sleeve, loosening the tape that held it to the wood.

"What's going on under there?" D.J. demanded, his voice oddly hoarse.

Not answering, Laini peeled the envelope away from the wide board it was anchored to and looked around for anything else Glen might have hidden there for safekeeping.

Nothing.

But this—what secrets did she hold in her hands?

When had Glen hidden the disk? And in the name of heaven, why here, in Murphy's room?

Was the disk what Virge—and last night's prowler—had been after?

Oh, heaven, she thought. What if the information on the disk linked Glen with a drug deal right here in Sycamore Point—exactly as Virge had intimated?

Realizing that she was shaking, she said huskily, "Pull me out, D.J."

His big hands clamped like a gentle vise over her hips and she was pulled easily between his spread legs until the top of her head cleared the aquarium base.

"Well, I'll be damned," D.J. muttered when he saw the computer disk in her hands.

"We wouldn't have finded it except for Frog!" Still clutching his pet, Murphy pranced around them as D.J. lifted Laini to her feet. "He jumped when I was putting him in his 'quarium and he finded it!"

"You'll have to reward him with an extra mealy-bug," Laini suggested.

Murphy beamed. "Can me and you and D.J. go get milk shakes?" Rewards, it seemed, were not for finders only.

"Sure can. If I can look at this—" she gestured with the floppy disk "—first."

Leaving D.J. and Murphy to reward Frog, she went to her own room rather than to Glen's computer and set up her trusty laptop model, which was compatible with Glen's PC.

Already familiar with Glen's word-processing program's codes, she had no trouble tapping into the disk—or losing herself in its contents.

Intending to scan rapidly for now, she soon found herself caught up in the flow of Glen's prose and dialogue. Before she knew it, she had read an outline and three chapters of a novel of the Washington political scene through which moved a shadowy figure involved in Caribbean drug trafficking, and realized it was a proposal for a book he appeared to be writing.

That Glen should have attempted such a book didn't surprise her. He'd had the talent, developed the skills, and as an investigative reporter, he'd surely racked up the experience to lend authenticity to the story.

But why would he risk everything by letting himself get involved, as Virge Weiss charged he had done, with an infamous drug czar very like the one in his manuscript? Why had he bid on that particular plane at the government auction and then flown it to Atlanta on the very weekend Weiss said the drug lord was meeting his "distributors" there?

She'd never been a great believer in coincidence.

Scrolling forward quickly, she could see that the novel was complete and that Glen had been awaiting word from his agent, who had been enthusiastic about the proposal. All that remained, from the looks of it, was a final polishing.

With an audible sigh, she turned off the laptop.

"Find anything?"

At D.J.'s soft-spoken question, Laini very nearly jumped out of her skin. She hadn't heard him enter the room.

"It's a novel—on Washington politics and drug smuggling—and his research notes. I'm not sure what else. I haven't been all through it yet. When did you come in?"

Leaning casually against the doorjamb, he shrugged. "A while ago. Are you ready for that milk shake? Murphy's chomping at the bit."

"Give me five minutes," she said, smiling at the phrase he'd used. Murphy seemed to be always chomping at the bit to go to the truck stop for milk shakes and video games.

When he'd gone, she removed the disk from the computer, tucked it back into its protective jacket and then placed it in the pocket of her shoulder bag where she carried valued notebooks and documents when she was working. No way was she going to risk either Weiss or the prowler finding it before she'd read every word and between the lines! She'd hidden information vital to a story she was working on in her computer, too—tucked it away in the middle of tedious research material or coded it into other copy—and Glen might have done the same things. She wasn't taking chances.

Always a quick-change artist, Laini peeled out of her jeans and sweater, showered, dressed in casual slacks and a dusky rose blouse, and applied eye shadow and lipstick, all in thirty seconds under the five minutes she'd promised.

With her bag slung over her shoulder, she found D.J. and Murphy in the library. Murphy was fidgeting, and D.J. had the phone propped against his ear. "Good deal, Harley, thanks," he finished as she entered the room, and hung up.

His appreciative glance swept over her, eliciting skirls of excitement in her. "You gave me ideas when I dragged you out from under that aquarium. Now you show up looking like this." A slow grin took possession of his face and her senses. "'Tain't fair, woman."

Laini went warm all over. *He* wasn't fair, making her feel as he did just by looking at her. She reminded herself there couldn't be a commitment between them for a long time, if ever. No matter how much she loved him, she was a long way from being ready to come home to Sycamore Point, even to be with him. Whereas he, she'd quickly realized, already thought of the small town as home.

"What good deal were you thanking Harley for?" she asked.

"He and Miss Annie just got back from spending the weekend at their daughter's and heard about last night's break-in. Harley offered to keep an eye on the place."

"That's good." She glanced at Murphy, who looked strange without Frog riding shotgun aboard clasped hands at his middle. "Ready to go?"

"Yes."

He sounded so like a diminutive D.J. that Laini's heart twisted. If she took him away from D.J. and Sycamore Point, she thought, it was going to break Murphy's heart. If she left him, it would break hers.

Not quite sure how Murphy had finagled Laini into sitting in the middle, D.J. was nevertheless grateful. Her shoulder brushed his, and her thigh was so close to his that he imagined he could feel her heat.

He could, he mused, take a steady diet of this for the rest of his life—Laini, him, Murphy, and sometime in the not-too-distant future, a child with Laini.

But first a wedding with Laini. He didn't care if they lived in a loft in SoHo, although he sure would miss Sycamore Point. It was the kind of place he'd like to grow old in—especially with Laini at his side.

"You're pensive." Laini broke the silence inside the wagon when they turned off Sycamore Point's main street onto the highway for the remaining short drive to the truck stop.

"What's pen–sive?" His blue eyes filled with the question, Murphy scooted forward on the leather seat until he could peer into their faces.

"It means I was thinking, Murph," D.J. answered, hoping the child would leave it there.

No such luck. "About marrying Laini?"

Horn blasting, an eighteen-wheeler whined past, causing D.J. to wonder what driving error he had committed, because Murphy's question had startled him.

"Good question."

Laini's tone was light but her face and throat were pink, D.J. noted. He grinned at her, and her flush deepened.

"I have to warn you, Murphy," she said. "I never talk marriage till I've had a chocolate shake."

"Betcha D.J. could—" Murphy began, his eyes dancing.

Laini's hand covered his mouth and he subsided, leaving D.J. wondering what he'd been about to say.

From the looks of the parking area, truckers from half the states east of the Mississippi had decided on lunch breaks at the same time, D.J. thought as he maneuvered the station wagon into a parking place between two semis. Dan Boles had a bearded driver backed up against his rig and was reading him the riot act about some infraction or other.

"See you inside, Murph," D.J. said when the boy opened the passenger door the moment the wagon stopped rolling.

"Can I have two scoops?"

"Whatever you want," Laini replied, smiling. "We'll be right in."

D.J. sent him off with a conspiratorial wink and a grin, then turned to Laini.

"Did you mean that about never talking marriage until you've had a chocolate shake?"

"No. But it might be fun if you worked at persuading me."

"Had something of the kind in mind," he admitted. "But since this is a public place, I guess we'd better talk. What do you think about that disk?"

Laini swallowed disappointment, chiding herself with *Well, what did you expect? A proposition? You've already had that: D.J.'s offer to take Murphy off your hands and wait around for you.*

Oh, sure, she thought. Wait around. He'd be in Sycamore Point with the boy she wanted to adopt, and she'd be in New York, a commodity marketed by the network's sales department and program people.

If only there was some way she could have it all!

"Hello in there?"

Fingers snapped in front of her, interrupting her musing. Laini glanced at D.J. A puzzled expression was on his face.

"Sorry." A faint chill went through her. "I was thinking."

"Must have been serious stuff. You looked like a kid who'd dropped her gum ball in the mud."

She felt like one, Laini reflected.

Collecting her thoughts, she told him how good the three chapters and outline of Glen's novel had seemed to her—and about the questions they'd raised in her mind.

D.J. listened without interrupting. Laini wondered what he was thinking. He and Glen had been through fire together, he'd told her. And yet, she mused with the part of her mind that wasn't focused on what she told him, Glen hadn't spoken to him about the plane—or about finding Murphy and planning to adopt him.

These were things, she thought, that best friends would have told each other.

Hadn't Glen trusted D.J. any longer? The suspicion sprang from some dark corner of her mind—and brought the roof caving in.

In the years when they'd covered guerrilla uprisings together, Glen had trusted D.J. with his life. So why hadn't he trusted him last summer? Especially if Glen had been involved in a DEA sting when D.J. was here, why hadn't Glen told him? There might have been some way D.J. could have helped.

People change, Laini, the little voice inside her warned. *Things happen that change them.*

Maybe one or more of those changes had taken place between Glen and D.J. Maybe it hadn't been Glen but D.J. who'd changed.

Uneasily she glanced at him. With his gaze focused on the ISP officer and the burly truck driver, he seemed totally oblivious to her, although she was seated so close beside him that she felt his heat.

"The thing that troubles me," she continued, wondering if he'd heard a word she had spoken, "is Glen going off like that without covering his bases. If he was going undercover, someone at the DEA knew about it—so Virge should have known it."

"I see your point," D.J. replied brusquely, when she was sure she couldn't stand the silence any longer. He seemed to shake himself mentally. "Let's go find Murph before he has chocolate shakes coming out his ears."

Laini slid across the seat, to find the passenger door opening before she touched the handle.

The ISP trooper and the bearded truck driver stood there, although she hadn't been aware of their approach.

"Miss Moran," the officer said as he gave her a hand out of the wagon, "Mr. George, here, has something I think you and Mr. Boone will find interesting." Boles nodded to D.J. as the latter strode around the front of the wagon and joined them.

The truck driver got right to the point. "I saw the kid get out of your wagon. Like I was telling the officer, I came through here a couple times a week, running between Chicago and points south. I saw that kid before and never forgot him." He continued with a flash of white teeth beneath a handlebar mustache. "He kind of sticks in your mind, you know? Especially when he took off from the car he was in like the devil himself was after him."

"When was that?" Laini and D.J. asked in unison.

"Late July. Had a load of melons from down south headed for Chicago when a flat brought me in here. Lucky for me, I guess. I found the refrigeration unit on the blink. I could have lost the whole damn load. Took a while to get on the road again."

"Anyway—" the trucker got back on track a split second before Laini would have interrupted "—that red-haired kid made my day."

"What about the driver of the car?" Laini asked.

"What kind of car?" D.J. inquired simultaneously.

"It was a beat-up little bug, two-tone blue and rust. Mean that literally—one fender was rusted clear through in places.

"I didn't get a good look at the driver. He was in the phone booth. Big man, though. Business type, I'd say—had on a short-sleeved white shirt. No coat, but it was hotter'n Hades that day." He shrugged. "The man left, I guess, while I was tinkering with the refrigeration. I had to add more freon."

The truck driver resettled his slouch hat on bushy blond hair. "Don't be too hard on the kid. The officer told me about him. Being on the road, a little kid like that could have run into any kind of weirdo." As though venting his spleen, he ground out the words: "You wouldn't believe the creeps on this road sometimes."

"I would believe," Laini told him, but didn't get into it. She'd had trouble dealing with her feelings as she'd listened to some of the experiences children had confided to her during the shooting of the documentary on homeless kids. She didn't want to think of any of those horror stories happening to Murphy.

After thanking the trucker, they talked for another few minutes with Trooper Boles, then entered the restaurant. Murphy, anchored to his shake glass by a straw, sat on the floor in front of a shelf of cartoon books.

"What do we do now?" Laini asked in a low voice.

"I don't know. I've never had a child before." D.J. squatted beside Murphy. "We've got to talk, Murph. Are you ready to go home?"

D.J. sounded so caring that she didn't remind him he didn't have a son, now; that she still hadn't made up her mind about Murphy. The look the boy gave him over the comic book and shake glass was so trusting, she felt the suspicion that lay so heavily in her mind lessen.

Surely a man who inspired such open confidence in a child could be trusted by the woman who loved them both?

"You asked her, didn't you?"

They were barely out the door, with Murphy between them, when the child popped the question.

If wedding bells could have been set off by a voice, Laini thought, the happiness in Murphy's would have done it. She wanted to hug him—even if, at the moment, marriage to D.J. seemed far away.

"No. But don't worry, Murph—" D.J. sounded as uneasy with the subject of marriage as she, Laini noticed "—I'll get around to it."

Laini caught one of Murphy's hands in hers. "We have to talk, honey," she began, moistening her lips.

"You changed your mind. You're not gonna keep me." He sounded as though her decision were a foregone conclusion, and his world had fallen apart—again.

"Of course we're going to keep you!" Laini burst out, hunkering down in front of him, her hands going to his bony shoulders, drawing him closer to her. "When I go back to L.A., you'll go with me—unless you'd rather stay here with D.J. for a while. Either way, I'm going to adopt you, just as Glen wanted me to do."

"I want you both to 'dopt me."

Glancing up at D.J., she found her senses instantly floundering at the expression she saw in his eyes.

Clearing his throat, he squatted on the parking-lot asphalt beside them. "I'm going to level with you, Murph. Laini and I may be a while getting together. She wants to adopt you before that, if she can, and the court's going to ask a lot of questions. They would ask a lot of questions even if we were married.

"But right now, she needs you to tell her things like who brought you to Sycamore Point." His voice was gentle but firm. "Can you tell her that, Murph?"

Murphy shifted his feet but didn't speak.

"Okay." D.J. sounded resigned. "Let me tell you something we heard just now from the man who was talking with Officer Boles in the parking lot."

Laini held her breath, expecting Murphy to bolt at the first mention of the big man in the rusty-fendered old Volkswagen.

Drinking in every word, he didn't flinch, nor did his gaze flicker from D.J.'s face. Laini's heart wrenched. Poor child. What dreadful experiences had he been through that he'd developed such iron control?

"Honey," she began softly when D.J. stopped talking, "if that man hurt you—"

"He didn't hurt me." His eyes pleaded with her. "Can I go now?"

When Laini nodded, he sped toward the station wagon.

Watching, D.J. shook his head. Holding out a hand to Laini, he drew her to her feet.

"Do you feel like we're in deep water?"

"And neither one of us can swim?"

There was no humor in his smile—nor in his voice. "Something like that."

Shoving both hands into the pockets of his windbreaker, D.J. stood looking at her, his blue eyes thoughtful. "The thing that bothers me is that if this guy didn't hurt him, why was Murphy as scared as that trucker said he seemed to have been?"

"Why," she echoed, "is he still so scared he jumps at shadows?"

"You got me," D.J. muttered.

Turning on his heel, he strode off toward the station wagon without a glance at her.

Wondering what had changed his mood so suddenly, Laini followed. Had what she'd said about Murphy jumping at shadows done it?

Mentally she shook her head. That didn't make sense. Even if Glen had done all the things Virge had accused him of, there was no way Murphy could have been involved, no way he could even have known.

In the wagon, D.J. pulled Murphy onto his lap and let him start the engine. And then he let him help drive home. Murphy was delighted; D.J. sat in stony silence.

Laini, feeling shut out, tended her own thoughts. What was it with D.J. that he'd gone from warm and caring to utterly remote?

The rapport she'd sensed between them the moment they'd met seemed to have vanished in a twinkling. She felt bereft, stripped of the airy hope that she and D.J. had been meant for each other—and meant for each other *now*, if only she could forget her burning ambition.

When the wagon stopped in the driveway behind Glen's car, she glanced at D.J. His jaw was clenched, and he appeared intent on some private nightmare she couldn't share.

What could it be, she wondered, that they couldn't talk about it? They'd discussed every facet—she had thought—of the case Virge presented against her brother; and had been drawn—inevitably, it seemed— toward Glen's guilt.

What could be worse than that?

You know what, the tiny inner voice informed her. *Finding out that D.J. may have betrayed Glen's trust. He might have done something that had led Glen to keep from him that he'd bought the plane and that he'd found Murphy.*

"Murph—" D.J. broke the silence "—why don't you go let Fruitful and the pups out while I talk to Laini for a sec?"

He sounded as serious as he looked, and Laini braced herself. For once, Murphy bounded out of the wagon without a word.

When he had disappeared around a corner of the house, D.J. continued: "It's about time we beefed up security around here, don't you think?"

"With Fruitful?" Laini managed not to laugh. The old hound was friendly to a fault.

A smile flickered across D.J.'s face. "You're forgetting something, aren't you? Fruitful's pups make a pretty good welcoming committee."

She would never forget, Laini thought. But this wasn't the time to let herself think about pitching down those front steps and lying so intimately atop D.J., while her senses and Fruitful's exuberant puppies went wild. She had trouble finding a reasonable answer.

"I guess they should've been out last night."

"Guess they should."

Was that disappointment she detected in his tone? What did he expect? That she fall all over him again—while he was holding himself so remote from her she could feel the chill?

"Virge," he began slowly, "might have looked good on his back in the mud with the pups licking the stuffing out of him."

Chapter Ten

Laini stared at him. *"Virge?"*

"Think about it. Murphy's petrified every time Virge is around. Virge—"

"That still doesn't explain what frightened Murphy in the first place. Remember, he said the man in the car didn't hurt him."

"—used to drive an old Volkswagen bug," D.J. went on as though she hadn't interrupted. His big hands gripped the steering wheel as if he feared the wagon would leap from under him although the ignition was shut off. "I never saw the vehicle myself, but Glen told me about it once. It was falling apart. With a family the size of his, it's doubtful he's replaced it on a DEA agent's salary."

Laini had had a lot of bad thoughts about Virge Weiss, but the worst of them had been that he was blind and stupid and stubborn where the charges against Glen were concerned.

She couldn't imagine Virge—with all those kids D.J. had said he was devoted to—doing anything that would have frightened Murphy so much he had leaped from the car and run to escape him—especially after Murphy had said he hadn't been hurt.

How had Virge and Murphy gotten together in the first place? she wondered, thinking how strange it seemed that Virge hadn't mentioned it. He'd seen Murphy at the memorial service; she was sure of it. Why hadn't Virge told them he'd met the boy before? It would have been the most natural thing in the world to have talked about when they were all trying to make conversation.

"Something tells me," she began speculatively as the pups and Fruitful set up a gleeful hue and cry out behind the house, "both Virge and Murphy have questions to answer."

Without making a response, D.J. opened the driver's-side door and got out, then reached across the seat for her hand.

"Unless you want a repeat of our first meeting—" he nodded toward the sounds of an approaching melee "—we'd better make a run for the house."

"Don't tempt me. Right now, I could use the diversion." *But dare not risk it,* she told herself.

With his hand on her arm, they barely made it inside before Murphy and his puppy storm-troopers charged the porch.

"Speckles wants to come in, too!"

"Not this time, honey." Laini held the door for him, then closed it in Speckles's face. They had begun the pup's housebreaking, and thus far it appeared a formidable task that needed her full attention. "We have to have a serious talk. Speckles wouldn't like it."

Watching his happiness fade and the fear that came into his expression, Laini hated herself. But Murphy had to be honest with them. She had an uneasy feeling he hadn't been.

Kneeling in front of him, she asked, "Why are you afraid of Mr. Weiss?"

"Don't know no Mr. Weiss."

"The man who was eating pie in the kitchen the night we turned Owl loose, Murph."

At D.J.'s words, Murphy edged away from them.

"Oh, honey," Laini said, her voice husky, "you don't have to be afraid to tell us *anything*!"

Fidgeting nervously, he barely whispered, "He had a suitcase full of money in his car."

Laini's breath caught in her throat. "You're sure?"

Murphy nodded solemnly. "I looked in it when he was talking on the phone at the truck stop. Soon as I seen the money, I ran."

"How did you happen to be in Virge's car, Murphy?"

A sneaker stubbed at the carpet. "He gave me a ride."

"From where?" D.J. prompted when Murphy gave no indication he planned to say anything further.

Murphy's shrug was eloquent, and unenlightening.

"Did you tell Glen?" Laini asked.

At the same time, D.J. asked, "Did you see Virge again before that night in the kitchen?"

"Didn't see him again, and I didn't tell nobody. I was scared to tell."

"Why, honey?"

"'Cause." Squirming, Murphy looked appealingly from one to the other of them. "Before she went away my momma used to say a lot of money meant a big drug buy was going down, and if I ever saw it, I was to run hard as I could. One night I never saw her again, and they tried to take me away but I ran."

Impulsively Laini pulled him to her. Kissing his freckle-spattered cheek, she whispered, "Thank you for telling us, Murphy."

"Yes, Murph—" D.J. gripped his shoulders "—thanks. You're a big help."

Murphy stood for a moment looking at them, his blue eyes wide and solemn. Then he sped off toward his room.

Watching him go, D.J. growled, "Next question: where the hell did Virge Weiss get a suitcase full of money?"

"And what was he doing with it in Sycamore Point?"

Laini's spirits, which had begun to lift, crashed. Oh, God. What if Weiss had gone into that phone booth to call Glen and ask directions to the house?

Had it been he who had provided the money Glen had used to buy the plane?

In the name of heaven, why? When he was a DEA agent dedicated to fighting drugs . . . Unless Glen had been working undercover, perhaps from the time he'd come home . . . setting the stage for when the time was right.

And it had been right?

"We're getting there, sweetheart." D.J.'s arm went around her shoulders, hugging her against his hard chest; bringing her thoughts back from speculation she couldn't share even with him.

"You don't know how I wish I could make it all go away," he continued. His thumb and forefinger lifted her chin so he could look into her eyes. "I think it's time we called in some muscle, love."

Laini had done a documentary, once, on a California stakeout that had netted a serial killer, and earlier in her career she had covered numerous other crime stories that had given her an inside look at police operations. But she had never been inside a house under surveillance when an arrest might be imminent.

The house being hers, and her brother having been somehow connected with the crime, made her doubly uneasy. She wished Glen had been more open with her.

She and Murphy were alone. Ostensibly D.J. was driving to Indianapolis where he was to catch a plane for D.C. He would—according to word that had been passed along, seemingly by accident, to Weiss—be gone for a day; at the most, two days.

Actually, he had joined the stakeout that he, Laini, Officer Boles and a drug task-force officer had planned that afternoon. Another officer, allegedly off duty, had spent the time drinking coffee and sharing drug-bust adventures with Weiss at a pancake-and-sausage place in Vincennes. Boles, as they'd planned, just happened to run into them there and dropped the bait.

The plan had sounded foolproof, and at first it had been relatively easy not to worry. She'd kept busy, printing off a copy of Glen's book and reading it in front of a fire in the library.

It had grown dark hours ago—an early, windy, rainy darkness that made her sorry for the men on stakeout; some of them were in the woods behind the house. Even with the fire crackling, she felt chilled to her marrow just from thinking about what might be about to happen.

What if something went wrong?

"Did you hear something?"

With those words, Murphy—curled up beside her on the sofa as he watched a nature program on public television—bolted upright.

"Just the wind," she replied, but strained her ears nevertheless.

"Can I go get Speckles?" At Boles's suggestion, they had returned Fruitful and the puppies to the kennel before dark.

She was trying to explain why he couldn't when the phone rang.

Instinctively she glanced at her watch. Almost ten o'clock.

Virge?

Renewed uneasiness darted through her. They hadn't expected him to call. Did he suspect something?

"John Baz here," the Washington editor barked when she answered. D.J. had told her Baz always barked. "Let me talk to D.J."

Cautiously she explained that D.J. wasn't there. "He may even be in Washington by now, Mr. Baz." *Don't take any chances, Laini. Weiss is cunning; he may have tapped the phone.* "I'm sure he'll call you."

"Glad to hear it. Something's happening over at the DEA."

"Like what?"

She thought he wasn't going to answer, but he said, "Hell, you're Glen's sister," as though reluctant to make the concession. "You're gonna know sooner or later. I've got D.J. working on special assignment, the Glen Moran story. He's probably told you. It'll earn him a Pulitzer, for sure."

"Like what, over at DEA?" Laini demanded, her heart sinking.

The Glen Moran story. A Pulitzer.

And D.J. hadn't told her.

"I can't tell you that," Baz answered. "You know the feds, Miss Moran. Play it close to the chest. That's their motto." She heard him suck in a breath. "Anything happening out there I should know?"

"Nothing," Laini lied. *Oh, D.J.! How could you?*

He hadn't returned to Sycamore Point to be with her and Murphy. He hadn't returned to help her clear

Glen's name. His story—*his damned story*—was all he cared about!

The rain had stopped around midnight, but the wind had picked up, driving a bone-biting chill through the windbreaker D.J. wore buttoned to his chin.

Someone had given him a government-issue slouch hat, but all it did was funnel the cold rain down the back of his neck. He hadn't been so uncomfortable since he and Glen had spent a winter covering the war in Afghanistan.

Why the hell didn't Virge come? Where was he?

An old hand at this sort of thing, Virge quite likely was gumshoeing around in the dark smelling out the setup, D.J. thought uneasily.

"A dark sedan just passed the newspaper building," Boles whispered as he materialized out of nowhere, walkie-talkie to his ear.

The fist in D.J.'s gut clenched tighter. He'd be glad when this was over.

How had he let Laini talk him into allowing her and Murphy to stay in the house alone? If anything happened to either one of them, he'd take Virge Weiss apart with his bare hands.

The voice on the walkie-talkie muttered in Boles's ear again; its tone was urgent though D.J. couldn't decipher the message.

"Let's go." Boles's calm had the strength of cold steel.

Moving out of their hiding place, they picked their way carefully through garden shrubbery, keeping low although it was so dark D.J. couldn't see his hand in front of his face.

Behind a tangle that last July when he'd been here had been a bower of blossoming red roses, a dozen feet from the window to Glen's room, Boles's hand on his arm signaled him to stop.

With his heart pumping what had to be pure adrenaline, D.J. went into the sprinter's crouch of his high-school days on the track team. When he heard a window open although he hadn't seen even a shadow move in the pitch-black darkness, he nearly leaped forward. Virge, light on his feet for a big man, hadn't made a sound as he came around the house.

Mere whispers of sound—reminding him of the quiet west Texas classrooms of his youth, in those early years before his mother had shipped him off to boarding school—grated on D.J.'s nerves.

Beside him, he sensed the trooper start his move toward the house, and D.J. followed him.

Inside Glen's room, a flashlight beam found the computer, and played over it.

Outside the window, D.J. watched with bated breath as a gloved hand snapped a disk out of its drive. Instantly the room was plunged into darkness again.

Unaware that he could move so fast and soundlessly, he was through the window and on the intruder's back before the man had a chance to move away from the computer.

"Damn you, Virge!"

Anger boiled up inside him, a tempest shattering his control into smithereens before its fury passed. His hands went instinctively to the man's throat.

"Glen trusted you, you lousy, no-good son of a—"

"Take it easy, Mr. Boone."

D.J. scarcely heard the officer or the expletives spit out at him in a high-pitched tenor voice he'd never heard before.

Whoever it was he'd wanted to strangle with his bare hands, it wasn't Virge.

"Well...well—" Wheezing and puffing, Virgil Weiss drew his overweight body laboriously through the window into the room. "Look who we got here! The kingpin's linchpin, no less!"

Inhaling sharply, Laini brought herself up short in the doorway.

What was going on? Virge was supposed to have been the one caught in the stakeout net, not sound as though he were ready to flap his wings and crow.

In the name of heaven, what was a drug king's second-in-command doing in Sycamore Point?

And stealing a computer disk that contained only nostalgia from the first—and probably only—issue of *Nostalgia, Pure and Simple* just didn't make sense.

A knot formed in the pit of her stomach. Oh, God. Was Virge right about Glen?

"Laini! D.J.! Come quick! He's getting away!"

Laini stopped breathing. Murphy had darted into his room to check on Frog. He wasn't supposed to be out there in the dark!

"*Yowwww!* Get in the car, you little—"

The snarled order was lost in Dan Boles's bellowed "Police! Halt!" as he went back out through the window, with D.J. close behind him.

Whirling, Laini ran for the front door.

Somewhere in the darkness at the front of the house, a car engine thundered into action and tires squealed.

"You've got to believe me, Laini—" Virgil Weiss's heavily jowled face was flushed to the point of apoplexy "—I wouldn't have had this happen even to get my hands on the kingpin himself."

Out of breath from having hustled his prisoner off to jail in custody of the heavily armed drug task-force officers who had taken part in the stakeout, he sounded as though his voice sloshed through emotion that was barely controlled.

Laini understood. She felt the same way, with scared-to-death added to it. Immediate pursuit of Murphy's kidnapper, and roadblocks set up, notwithstanding, the speeding sedan with Murphy in it seemed to have vanished from the face of the earth.

"If that kid gets hurt—"

"If that kid gets hurt," D.J. echoed, cutting in, "the bastard who does it won't see the inside of a jail if I get to him first. Or get out of one if I can get to him in his cell."

"Let me finish, Deej."

Virge sucked in a breath that seemed to whistle all the way to his lungs. Laini glanced quickly at him. Oh, heavens. Was the man going to hyperventilate?

"If anything happens to Murphy," Virge continued, his tone gone taut and raspy, "Glen's going to kill me."

Laini inhaled so sharply it hurt. *"What did you say?"*

The DEA agent shifted uneasily on his big feet. In spite of her shock, the movement reminded Laini of Murphy when he faced a sticky question he didn't quite know how—or want—to answer.

"Glen's alive, Laini."

Staring at Virge, Laini felt a surge of anger begin deep within her. How dare he let her believe Glen was dead! Let her grieve—let Murphy think he'd lost his best friend in all the world!

"This had better be good, Virge," D.J. said warningly. A dark scowl knitted his bristling mahogany eyebrows. "You put Laini through hell, man—to say nothing of Murphy and me. It better be worth it."

Breathing more or less evenly again, Laini managed to ask, "Is he—was he hurt?"

Weiss exhaled audibly, sounding, Laini thought, as though the weight that had been lifted from his shoulders was as great as the one that had gone from her heart.

"Glen thought it was worth it. And no, Laini—" he answered both their questions in the same breath "—he wasn't seriously hurt. He sprained an ankle when he landed, and got a few scratches and bruises."

A chuckle rustled in his throat. "Glen must have been wearing a rabbit's foot. Bailing out in that storm the way he did, he could have been killed."

"Where is he now?"

"I can't tell you that, Laini."

The chunk of ice the size of Mendenhall Glacier that had been in her chest since Murphy's kidnapping got larger. Glen was in danger!

And Murphy— Oh, God, she thought. What might be happening to Murphy?

What might *already* have happened to him?

The devil's drum of her fear picked up its tempo.

"What can you tell us?"

Looking uncomfortable, Weiss answered, "An ongoing investigation is classified. You know that, Laini."

Surprise went through her. In the wink of an eye, he had shifted vocal fonts, from good ole boy, her brother's friend, to the no-nonsense, by-the-book DEA agent he'd been at their first meeting. Glancing at D.J., she saw only a perplexity in his expression that matched her own.

Laini's frustration flared. "Oh, come off it, Virge. You're dealing with a couple of pros. How long do you think it's going to take the media in Vincennes to pick up on who you've got in jail and that a child was taken hostage by a second man you didn't even suspect was at the scene?" Her blood congealed in her vessels, but she forced herself to go on. "How long before they'll tie it all to Glen?"

"Gonna be a great story, Virge." D.J.'s soft Texas drawl was velvet over steel.

Laini's heart wrenched. His Glen Moran story that was going to earn him a Pulitzer, his editor had said.

Well, she hoped he got it....

"All right, all right—" Weiss conceded at least partial defeat "—the whole thing was Glen's idea, worked out with Washington. He would come back here, make it look good, put out feelers. Getting his hands on the plane was a break he hadn't expected, but he felt—I guess we all did—it was worth the risk. I fetched the money—"

"Enter Murph," D.J. said.

Virge nodded. "Picked him up this side of Chattanooga. Couldn't get him filled up; I'd swear we stopped at every McDonald's from there to here."

In spite of herself, Laini smiled.

Virge went on talking.

"...Laini Moran, reporting for..."

Leaning forward, Laini snapped off the television set.

How had she managed to sound so professional, show such presence in front of the camera? She'd felt neither professional nor in control, wanting to shout to the world that her brother was alive and to plead with, cajole and threaten the man who had kidnapped Murphy.

She could do neither. Glen's "death" was part of what Weiss had called Plan B, which had been put into operation when something had mysteriously gone

wrong with the plane Glen had been flying to Atlanta. Both engines and the communications gear had
conked out at the same time, Weiss had explained.

And she dared not put Murphy further at risk by
berating his kidnapper on nationwide television. The
man had to have been frightened and desperate and
not thinking straight. Heaven knew what he might do.

Although she had been on the run all day, she still
couldn't relax. She'd spent the hours interviewing,
pulling her story together—while trying to keep her
anguish over Murphy locked inside her—and had arrived home a short time earlier from Terre Haute,
where she'd taped the news segment.

"It's been fifteen hours," she said, jumping up and
crossing the room to the window. Darkness outside
concealed dragons she wasn't sure she wanted to deal
with, so she turned back to D.J.

"Fifteen hours, seventeen minutes and—" his
glance dropped to his watch "—thirty-seven seconds."

He sounded as though they'd been the longest fifteen hours, seventeen minutes and thirty-seven seconds of his life. As they had been of hers. "Oh, D.J.,"
she whispered, "what if we never see him again?"

Gentle hands turned her into his arms, but it didn't
help. She'd had her miracle: Glen was alive, when
she'd said goodbye to him in her heart. She couldn't
expect another one.

Even if they found Murphy safe and sound, her
world would never hold the pleasure she'd come to
expect of it. Murphy would be Glen's son, not hers.

Not hers and D.J.'s.

Glen and some woman lucky enough to marry him would raise Murphy in Sycamore Point with the love and sense of family that Glen had trusted her to provide. While she— *While you what?* demanded the little voice she called her inner self. *Go back to being a whole lot lonely?*

"Oh, D.J.—" her face pressing against his chest stifled a moan "—why couldn't it have been different for us?"

Chapter Eleven

Laini—"

More asleep than awake after hours of tossing and turning, Laini struggled through fog that seemed reluctant to let her go.

Visions of Murphy and D.J. and the life they might have had together in Sycamore Point danced through her head, tormenting her because it wasn't going to be that way—for her. She wasn't going to have either D.J. or Murphy, and—she'd come to realize—she was going to miss them both terribly.

"Sis?"

"Sorry to have put you through all that," Glen said, much later, when he, Laini and D.J. were seated at the kitchen table drinking coffee. Glen had explained a lot of what had happened, corroborating what Virge had told them and what they'd figured out for themselves.

Leaning over, Laini gently touched the ugly bruise on his temple.

"You're forgiven—now," she told him, smiling. "Although I don't mind telling you, when Virge first told us you were alive and hiding out while I went through hell grieving for you, I was mad enough to have killed you myself."

"I knew you would be, and I can't say I blame you. But, dammit, Sis, we'd gone too far to back down. That plane wasn't supposed to crash. We had to come up with an alternate plan in a hurry—something that would let the kingpin—" he uttered a name so big in international drug trafficking that a chill skirled through Laini "—think I had died in the crash but may have left evidence to link me to his operation, so he'd send his bird dog after it."

"Enter Virge," D.J. drawled. "Well, let me tell you buddy, Virge did a good job. He damn near had *me* believing you'd gone over the edge somewhere between Afghanistan and Sycamore Point."

Glen gulped coffee. "That was the idea from the first, even before I left Washington. Settle into the old hometown, then appear to get antsy—but only in the right places, so word would trickle through channels. You know—let it be known that I wanted in on the action, on the big, easy money.

"It's happened before, believe me. Straight arrows tired of seeing the big money that's to be had from moving drugs and deciding what the hell, they might just as well have a piece of the action as the next guy.

"In my case, we had to make it look and sound good enough to be true without overdoing it. What good's a Pulitzer in Sycamore Point, Indiana? Why shouldn't I cash in on some of the big, easy drug money I'd seen laundered? Incidentally, Sis," he interjected, "there's nothing hidden in that novel or on the disk that'll shake up the drug world. It was just important that the big boy thought there might be, so he'd come after it."

Hearing the words, and the ease with which he uttered them, Laini shuddered inwardly. Had her brother actually put his life on the line so casually? And expected the plan to work without a hitch?

"Virge and one or two others," Glen continued, "fed the bait into channels that the drug lord uses for recruits. Before we knew it, we were in business. The DEA came up with the money, and Virge brought it up here. Finding Murphy, naturally, was not planned for. But we were so close that I figured I'd take care of him and after my work with Virge was over, I'd help settle Murphy's future. I bid on the plane and was all set to meet the big man at his distributors' convention in Atlanta. Word was I was to open up a new territory. But the plane wasn't supposed to crash! Everything was in tip-top shape, from the tracking gear that'd been installed on down. And yet, the whole shebang shut down at once. Engines, radio, hydraulic system." He swore and shook his head. "Just like someone had pulled the plug."

"Maybe someone did. Had you thought of that?" Laini asked. Suddenly, things that she hadn't understood took on a new meaning. Murphy must have seen the suitcase of money Virge had brought for Glen to bid on the aircraft.

"Sure, I've thought of it. Until I saw you on TV and realized what I'd done to Murphy, I thought of little else. Drug traffickers are a vindictive lot, and I've helped put a few of them away. They'd undoubtedly find great satisfaction in taking me out."

There was a pause, during which he stared into his empty coffee mug, seeming scarcely to notice when D.J. got up and filled it again.

"But this was worth the risk—it was to net us a big one."

Swallowing coffee that Laini suspected he didn't taste, Glen lifted a bleak gaze to hers. "God, Laini—" a hand brushed the groan off his lips "—if anything's happened to Murphy—"

Laini's heart went out to him. She knew the dread he was feeling. If anything had happened to Murphy, she didn't know what *she* would do, either.

"Orders are to stick with you, Miss Moran, right up to time to get us to tape-edit before airtime," the young cameraman stated.

"Good," Laini said, smiling at him. She suspected he was an apprentice, possibly a student working part-time at the Terre Haute television station that was affiliated with the same network as her station in Los Angeles. She liked his enthusiasm.

They had filmed Glen talking with Trooper Boles and the sheriff and were waiting outside the county's law-enforcement center for "the kingpin's linchpin" to emerge with his attorney, en route to a court appearance that would set bond. Which, Boles had grumbled, would be "plunked down like it's peanuts, putting the bastard back on the streets to do it again."

The cameraman sidled closer, camcorder at the ready. "See the guy on the courthouse steps? In the sheepskin and pretending not to look this way?"

Something in his tone sent excitement leaping through Laini. "Yes."

"He owns an old farmhouse up in the river bottom. Last summer there was enough marijuana growing 'round it to send me through college and graduate school if the cops hadn't trashed it. He seems mighty interested in the goings-on over here. Can't help wondering if he's waiting for our man."

"Are you getting him on tape?" She'd just realized his camera was running, although he wasn't looking into the viewfinder. It was a trick she'd seen before.

"Better believe it!"

"Good." Laini forced herself to continue breathing normally. "Can you get us out to his place?"

"Now?"

"Now," she echoed. "Leave your camera running, so he won't suspect you've photographed him."

Tucking an arm companionably through his, Laini gave him a dazzling smile for the watching man's benefit and they started walking toward the car with Television News emblazoned on its side. There were more important things to do than videotaping a prisoner who'd thumbed his nose at the law before.

A chance—however slim—of finding Murphy was at the top of her list.

Laini's heart sank at her first glimpse of the ramshackle shotgun house. Obviously abandoned and falling apart for many years, it bore the marks of vandals and the river that flooded the surrounding bottomland with regularity.

"For his sake," the young cameraman muttered, "I almost hope we don't find the kid in there. The place looks like a rat harbor."

Shuddering, Laini didn't respond.

As the car moved slowly toward the house, her glance searched for any signs of activity. She saw nothing. But another car had been there recently— since the night of Murphy's abduction, when it had rained. Tire prints marked the dirt road.

Tattered curtains and shredded blinds flapped in the wind that blew through the shattered windows. The front door hung askew on one hinge, leaving the way open for animals from the woods that verged on the burned-over marijuana plots to enter the house at will.

Laini shivered. Not even a monster would hold a small boy hostage in a place like this!

"Got some bad vibes about the place." The cameraman glanced nervously about as he drove toward it. "Wouldn't like to be caught out here in the middle of nowhere by the wrong people."

Although she agreed with him, Laini couldn't bring herself to admit it aloud. "Stop here and start shooting. Pan around to get some good overall shots. Around back, too."

Nodding, the cameraman stopped the car and reached into the back seat for his equipment.

Fumbling in her shoulder bag for the small container of mace she always carried for emergencies, Laini dropped the bag on the floorboards and the mace into her jacket pocket.

"You ever had to use that stuff?" The photographer sounded as though he might be having second thoughts about having accompanied her.

"Oh," Laini began offhandedly, "once or twice. Always be prepared. That's my motto." She hadn't sounded nearly as blasé as she'd hoped.

Having some second thoughts of her own, Laini walked toward the rickety steps that were all that remained of a front porch that once had spanned the front of the narrow building. Although it was only a few miles from Sycamore Point, this place seemed to her to be in another world. Anything could happen here, she guessed—and probably had.

Chewing the inside of her bottom lip to stop it from trembling, she pushed at the sagging door. It opened with a screech of its single remaining rusted hinge.

The small room she entered was empty, its floor carpeted with dust that had been marked by animal tracks. Holding her breath because of the stench, she hurried through a doorless entryway into another room, also empty of furnishings, its windowpanes broken like those at the front of the house. A sharp wind blew in and penetrated straight through her flesh to her bones.

There was a closed door directly in front of her. And it was a very solid-looking door.

In this wreck of a house?

Sensing the cameraman behind her, she half turned, holding a finger to her lips.

With camera poised and running, he nodded.

The door jerked open before she could touch the knob.

"Ho—" A man holding a gun pointed directly at her, chuckled. "Glen Moran's kid, and now, Glen Moran's sister."

Murphy came from behind him in a flying-squirrel leap.

"Murph, you're a hero," D.J. said later that evening after Laini's broadcast of the boy's rescue had ended. "But if you ever pull a stunt like that again, I'll turn you over my knee and tan your backside."

Murphy shot him a look of utter disbelief. "You saw him on the TV! He was going to shoot Laini!"

"Not after your Superman tackle, Murph. I owe you for that and I always will." A raspy note tugged at his voice as he glanced at Laini, who had watched the taped segment with them as though she were in another world.

Wishing he knew what she was thinking, D.J. dragged his gaze from her face and continued, "Just don't go out any more windows, the way you did the other night, when there's a roomful of policemen to give chase. You could have been killed."

"He was getting away." Murphy sounded as though that made his recklessness all right.

"You still could have gotten killed," D.J. repeated.

"But I didn't."

Squirming deeper into the sofa, where he sat between Laini and Glen, Murphy readjusted Frog. He looked, D.J. thought, as though he hadn't a worry in the world.

Lord, how he wanted that to be true for all of them; but, he reminded himself, life wasn't like that. With Glen back, the whole picture had changed. Murphy would be Glen's child, not his. Not his and Laini's—however far apart they seemed to be on working anything out between them.

Which was the way it should be, he reflected. Glen was settled in Sycamore Point, which was a great place for a kid.

He wasn't settled anywhere, although Glen had offered him his present room in the Moran house for as long as he wanted it. Tempted, D.J. knew he wouldn't accept the invitation for longer than an occasional vacation.

Watching Murph grow up from a distance, seeing him now and then, would be better than nothing—he guessed.

Laini found D.J. alone at the breakfast table the next morning, although Miss Annie had set a festive table for four. A low silver bowl held one of the housekeeper's prized African-violet plants in full flower. Haviland china and antique silverware Laini couldn't remember having seen out of the dining-room cabinets except for cleaning, graced the table.

Another silver bowl containing another blossoming violet sat on the side table near the door to the kitchen. Tantalizing smells rose from beneath the covers of heated serving dishes.

Laini smiled and said good-morning. "Where is everyone?"

Murphy was usually first at the table, and Glen hadn't answered when she'd tapped lightly on his door, across from her own.

"Out looking for Owl," D.J. answered with a grin. "Murph thought he heard a few hoots in the night, so Glen took him on an owl hunt before breakfast. Murph thinks Owl was welcoming Glen home. Glen said great, they'd go renew an old acquaintance."

How like Glen, Laini thought as she went to the side table and picked up a heated plate.

"Murph's in seventh heaven."

Forcing a smile that D.J. couldn't see because she couldn't bring herself to turn from the serving table and meet his eyes, she said lightly, "I can imagine."

"So why do I feel like the bottom has just fallen out of my life?"

Laini served herself by rote—melon, eggs Benedict, toast. Carrying her plate back to the table, she forced herself to look at him. "I thought it was the roof that caved in."

"And you feel like a traitor?"

"Something like that," Laini confessed, sitting down and folding her hands around the cup he'd filled with coffee for her.

Eyes on the steam that rose in a lazy spiral from the coffee in the dainty cup, she continued, "I know Murphy needs Sycamore Point, and this house, and Frog, and Fruitful and the pups.... I know he needs the love and companionship Glen can give him. I'm glad. I want what's best for Murphy. But—" The sigh that whispered past her lips was audible, revealing. "I'm going to miss him."

"And Sycamore Point, this house, Frog, Fruitful and the pups?" D.J.'s voice bordered on hoarseness.

"We saw Owl! He was up in a tree!"

Murphy's gleeful announcement saved her from answering—when she wasn't sure she could have spoken steadily if her life had depended on it.

"We saw him!" Murphy repeated, bubbling over with excitement. Practically dancing up and down, he asked, "Want to come see him, Laini? D.J.? He's close to where we turned him loose!"

"Laini and D.J. can see him later," Glen said, grinning at the two of them. "That was a nesting tree I showed you, Murphy. I bet that's where Owl lives. You watch it next spring, and you might see some young owls."

Laini felt misty inside. She might miss Murphy like crazy, but this was where he belonged. How many owls' nesting trees could she point out to him in New York?

So let him show you this one. It'll be an experience to treasure when you're homesick for what might have been.

Laini was on her feet before common sense put the inner voice back in its place. She reached out to Murphy. "Let's go. Breakfast can wait."

"Will you drive me to school if I miss the bus?"

"Yes."

Holding on to her hand, Murphy dragged her after him toward the kitchen and the back door.

She didn't see the glances Glen and D.J. exchanged.

Chapter Twelve

When Laini returned from chauffeuring Murphy to school, she found Glen and D.J. nursing thick ironstone mugs of coffee in front of the library fireplace.

"Got a deal for you, Sis," Glen announced, greeting her with a gesture to join them.

They looked so good sitting there, and appeared so pleased about something, that Laini couldn't help smiling. "This had better be good. I talked to my Los Angeles news editor yesterday from Terre Haute. I'll be leaving for L.A. tomorrow, to get ready for the move to New York."

There. She'd said it, made the announcement she had dreaded making.

"That's good," Glen responded, sounding extremely pleased. "My agent called. He wants the book as soon as I get through polishing it, plus he thinks he can sell a television special on what he calls 'The Glen Moran Story.' "

Brown eyes, so like her own, twinkled. "I told him to go for it, as long as it airs on your station's network, you have production control, and they give you a leave after you finish it so you can come home for three or four months with Murphy and me. Do we have a deal?" he finished.

Laini had a little trouble getting her breath back. When she did, she cried, "We have a deal—Oh, Glen, yes, we have a deal!"

Setting his now empty coffee mug down, Glen rose and plunked a brotherly kiss on her cheek. "I've got one more thing to wrap up before I settle down for good." He grinned. "Just Murphy and me, and Frog, and Fruitful."

Laini felt her elation slipping, just a little. She was being eased out of Murphy's life, and it was her own fault. Both Glen and D.J. thought her career was the most important thing in her universe...and all of a sudden she wasn't sure that it was.

"That story I told you about down in Marazán," Glen continued. "I need to get back down there. D.J. will be here with Murphy. Sis...maybe they can visit you some weekends in New York."

She *should* be happy....

When Glen had gone off to his room to call Baz, his editor in Washington, Laini went into the kitchen to pour herself a mug of coffee. To quiet her quivering insides, she told herself. How could she feel so empty, so as if she'd been robbed of something she wanted so badly she could taste it?

Nothing had changed. She still had what she had wanted most for all these years: the network anchor slot, with Glen's "Glen Moran Story" as a plum freshly fallen into her eager hands.

Eager hands? She looked at them. Trembling hands would be more like it. To stop the trembling, or at least to hide it, she wrapped both hands around the hot ironstone mug.

"Laini," D.J. said softly from behind her.

She turned to find him standing so close his very essence filled her nostrils, was drawn deep into her lungs. Why didn't it strengthen her, as it always had before?

Because she was losing him, too?

"Glen's not the only one who's been thinking, Laini." His big hands closed over her shoulders. "You know how I feel about this place, Laini. I'd like nothing better than to spend the rest of my life here ... unless it's spending it with you.

"Soon as Glen's home for good, Laini—" very gently he turned her to face him, the mug of steaming coffee still gripped in both her hands "—I'm coming to New York. I want to marry you, love, but I want you any way you'll have me."

Blue eyes probed her brown ones. "Sure as there's a God in Texas, Laini, I love you and will till the day I die. And I will follow you to the ends of the earth—"

"Don't make rash statements, Boone." She tried to sound flip, as though her world hadn't suddenly turned upside down and, in righting itself, sent her well-ordered plan for her career careening off into outer space.

Grinning, D.J. took the mug from her and set it carefully on the kitchen counter. "It's not a rash statement. I've given it a lot of thought." His grin broadened. "Like from the moment that speckled pup did me the biggest favor of my life."

His eyes devoured her. "I'm not the great romantic when it comes to words, love. I just want to love you, take care of you, share the good and the bad . . ."

Laini wasn't sure she'd heard all the words—or had to hear them all. They could make it work—*she* could make it work! She could feed things to the network through that station in Terre Haute, maybe even do "The Glen Moran Story" from there. . . .

She went into his arms as though she intended to stay there forever. "And I want to love you," she whispered, "take care of you, share the good and the bad. Not in New York," she murmured against his lips, "but right here in Sycamore Point. Oh, D.J.! I've so much to tell you!"

But she didn't. Not for a long, wonderful time.

The world, it suddenly seemed, could wait.

* * * * *

Watch for CRANE'S MOUNTAIN, coming from Silhouette Romance in December.

Silhouette Special Edition®

Now appearing
in a special return engagement, Nora Roberts's
bestselling 1988 miniseries featuring

THE O'HURLEYS!
Nora Roberts

Book 1 **THE LAST HONEST WOMAN** *Abby's Story*
Book 2 **DANCE TO THE PIPER** *Maddy's Story*
Book 3 **SKIN DEEP** *Chantel's Story*

And making his debut in a brand-new title, a very special
leading man . . . Trace O'Hurley!

Book 4 **WITHOUT A TRACE** *Trace's Tale*

In 1988, Nora Roberts introduced THE O'HURLEYS!—a close-knit
family of entertainers whose early travels spanned the country. The
beautiful triplet sisters and their mysterious brother each experience
the triumphant joy and passion only true love can bring, in four books
you will remember long after the last pages are turned.

Don't miss this captivating miniseries—a special collector's edition
available now wherever paperbacks are sold.

OHUR-1A

Double your reading pleasure this fall with two Award of Excellence titles written by two of your favorite authors.

Available in September

DUNCAN'S BRIDE
by Linda Howard
Silhouette Intimate Moments #349

Mail-order bride Madelyn Patterson was nothing like what Reese Duncan expected—and everything he needed.

Available in October

THE COWBOY'S LADY
by Debbie Macomber
Silhouette Special Edition #626

The Montana cowboy wanted a little lady at his beck and call—the "lady" in question saw things differently....

These titles have been selected to receive a special laurel—the Award of Excellence. Look for the distinctive emblem on the cover. It lets you know there's something truly wonderful inside!

DUN-1

From *New York Times* Bestselling author
Penny Jordan, a compelling novel of ruthless passion
that will mesmerize readers everywhere!

Penny Jordan

Silver

Real power, true power came from
Rothwell. And Charles vowed to have it,
the earldom and all that went with it.

Silver vowed to destroy Charles, just as surely and
uncaringly as he had destroyed her father; just as he had
intended to destroy her. She needed him to want her . . .
to desire her . . . until he'd do anything to have her.

But first she needed a tutor: a man who wanted no one.
He would help her bait the trap.

Played out on a glittering international stage,
Silver's story leads her from the luxurious comfort of
British aristocracy into the depths of adventure,
passion and danger.

AVAILABLE NOW!

 **HARLEQUIN**

Win 1 of 10 Romantic Vacations and Earn Valuable
Travel Coupons Worth up to $1,000!

Inside every Harlequin or Silhouette book during September, October and November, you will find a PASSPORT TO ROMANCE that could take you around the world.

By sending us the official entry form available at your favorite retail store, you will automatically be entered in the PASSPORT TO ROMANCE sweepstakes, which could win you a star-studded London Show Tour, a Carribean Cruise, a fabulous tour of France, a sun-drenched visit to Hawaii, a Mediterranean Cruise or a wander through Britain's historical castles. The more entry forms you send in, the better your chances of winning!

In addition to your chances of winning a fabulous vacation for two, valuable travel discounts on hotels, cruises, car rentals and restaurants can be yours by submitting an offer certificate (available at retail stores) properly completed with proofs-of-purchase from any specially marked PASSPORT TO ROMANCE Harlequin® or Silhouette® book. The more proofs-of-purchase you collect, the higher the value of travel coupons received!

For details on your PASSPORT TO ROMANCE, look for information at your favorite retail store or send a self-addressed stamped envelope to:

PASSPORT TO ROMANCE
P.O. Box 621
Fort Erie, Ontario L2A 5X3

ONE PROOF-OF-PURCHASE

3-CSR-2

To collect your free coupon booklet you must include the necessary number of proofs-of-purchase with a properly completed offer certificate available in retail stores or from the above address.

© 1990 Harlequin Enterprises Limited